RIKKI FULTON'S
REVEREND I. M. JOLLY

BOOK 2

RIKKI FULTON'S
REVEREND I. M. JOLLY

BOOK 2

ONE DEITY AT A TIME,
SWEET JESUS

Tony Roper

BLACK & WHITE PUBLISHING

First published 2003
by Black & White Publishing Ltd
99 Giles Street, Edinburgh EH6 6BZ

ISBN 1 902927 85 0

British Library Cataloguing in Publication Data:
A catalogue record for this book is available
from the British Library.

Cover photograph: Stephen Kearney
Cover design: www.hen.uk.com

Printed and bound by Creative Print & Design

Introduction

BY **RIKKI FULTON** OBE

I would like to thank my loyal parishioners, all four of them, namely, Jean, Margaret, Walter and Mary, for raising enough money to buy one copy of my dear friend Tony Roper's book – to share between them. Their generosity knows no bounds and, hopefully, they'll let *me* see it when they've finished.

For myself, I am happily convalescing in a nursing home, and I do mean happily. I've never seen so many pretty nurses, especially the red-haired one.

I am here as the result of one of the world's greatest health hazards – Ephesia's cooking. The very thought of it makes me feel ill again so, if you'll excuse me, I'll just ring for the redhead to arrange my pillows and soothe my brow.

Oh, I've just had a wonderful idea! SHE could buy Tony's book, *One Deity at a Time, Sweet Jesus*, and read it to me. What a beautiful thought!

Yours in joyful anticipation
and with good wishes to you, dear reader,
I. M. Jolly

Written by Kate, because she has the pencil, but dictated by

Rikki

To Susie

RIKKI FULTON'S
REVEREND I. M. JOLLY

BOOK 2

GENESIS V1

God: *Make thee an Ark of gopher wood*

Noah: *What?*

God: *Gopher wood*

Noah: *OK. I'll be back in ten minutes*

HELLO AGAIN.

Once more, I've decided to let you in on the incredible, improbable and extraordinary lifestyle of a typical Church of Scotland minister.

As I sit here in my favourite chair, looking at the portrait of Her Majesty on the wall in my cosy little room in Balmoral Castle – a room that I like to call the study but everyone else calls the dungeon – I must admit to a feeling of awe and wonderment at this interwoven tapestry that is life.

It amazes me that it was only last year I was invited, with my dear wife Ephesia, at the specific request of Her Majesty, to be her beacon in the sea of confusion that life can often be. Indeed, I have become such a beacon for her, I once overheard a member of Her Majesty's staff state that my study was like a lighthouse. I'm sure that's what they meant. Unfortunately, due perhaps to a speech impediment, it sounded like a description of what, in polite society, is called 'the smallest room'.

You may remember, if you have read my last epistle, *How I Found God and Why He Was Hiding From Me* – if you haven't, I think you should – it was after my hair-raising adventures with a poor unfortunate creature who, through no fault of his own but purely due to a cruel twist of fate, was cast in the mould of villain, that I arrived at Balmoral. This hapless and star-crossed innocent victim of life harboured an unreasonable hatred for me because I was a shining example to humanity whereas he was a transvestite nutter who thought he was Jack the Ripper and was hell-bent on trying to do me in.

What a fruitcake! I mean to say, we can all lose the plot now and then but this balloon was obviously certifiable – a one hundred per cent dough-ball who should have had the two spherical objects that dangle from his manhood cut off and thrown to the . . . Sorry, I seem to have digressed into an avenue that, as a man of God, I perhaps shouldn't have. Anyway, it was after that regrettable affair that I was invited to become the Queen's Minister in Scotland by the Church of Scotland's representative, the Very Reverend Ewen Mee.

Understandably, I thought that I had seen the end of surprises and adventures for my allotted time on this planet. It is, therefore, with utter astonishment that I now put pen to paper again to record what seems to me to be an even more bizarre series of bewildering happenings.

It all began only a month ago when I received another visit from the Very Reverend Ewen Mee. I was in the castle gardens tending to a group of sick cyclamens. The reason the cyclamens were sick was due to my wife Ephesia deciding to help them grow strong and vigorous by applying a fertiliser of her own devising that she had been nursing along in her compost heap. Ephesia has her own rules when it comes to compost. Unlike the prevailing wisdom of letting the manure rot down until there is virtually no distinguishing feature or odour left, she feels that the fresher the manure, the more beneficial it will be. On what was an unusually hot, sultry day the beneficence was there for everyone to smell and the cyclamens were so intoxicated by all this goodness they were flattened.

The castle gardener along with the entire castle staff informed me they were going to bestow a similar fate on Ephesia. In a reckless bid to avert an unfair bout of fisticuffs between the staff and Ephesia (there were only eight of them, not a serious match for her), I promised to restore the cyclamens to their original state. It was as I was bending to retrieve the clothes peg, which had fallen from my nose, that I heard the strangled vowels of Ewen Mee strafe their way across the garden. He was one of those people who you find it very hard to discern what age they are – he looked fifteen, approaching fifty. He was also extremely challenged in a vertical sense. Indeed, his feet appeared to dangle just above the ground, even when he was standing, which is unusual.

'Eh say, Jolly, meht Eh hev eh word with you?' he called out in a voice that tried desperately not to use the 'a' vowel. As he drew level, I noticed that his face was flushed and abnormally moist. Moreover, the lenses in his spectacles were steaming up. I also noticed his nose had begun to twitch and bleed slightly.

'In the name of Our Saviour's Memmy, ken you not take something for thet, Jolly? What hev you been eating? It smells like raw sewage.'

'Well, it more or less is raw sewage,' I replied, noticing that his image was starting to shimmer due to the heat rising from the ground and Ephesia's compost.

'Hev you completely lost your mend? Whe er you eating raw sewage? Eh realise your wife's not the most ettrective of women but there er more pleasant ways to poison yourself then thet,' he choked whilst stuffing a handkerchief up his nose to staunch the blood which was now flowing more freely. 'Eh hev to tell you, mehn, you er completely rencid.'

'It's not me that's rancid,' I corrected him, 'it's the flowers.'

'What er they?' he asked, gazing at the flattened flowers with ill-disguised rancour. 'Let us hope thet they're en endangered species.'

I decided it wasn't worth the bother of explanations and assured him, with a degree of accuracy, that they were unlikely to survive the night.

'Thenk the Lord for thet,' he said wringing out his hand-kerchief. 'Es you ken see, Jolly, Eh em in eh certehn emount of distress here. Would it be possible to evecuate this haven of excrementia for somewhere less offensive to the senses. There must be a pigsty or a public levetory free somewhere, surely?' His voice contained more than a hint of sarcasm.

11

Of course, in defence of Ephesia's compost, I was tempted to join in trading insults and crush him with a telling phrase that would leave him speechless but I decided against this action because, frankly, it was beneath me and, even more frankly, I couldn't think of any telling phrases.

'There should be a room free somewhere in the castle,' I informed him. 'Follow me.'

We set off at pace across the lawn due to the fact that Ewen Mee was in a desperate hurry to get away from the, shall we say, smell of the countryside? In fact, he left me behind in his haste and, eventually, I lost sight of him altogether as he disappeared into the castle. Fortunately, the trail of blood from his nose was clearly visible and afforded me an excellent opportunity to practise my long forgotten skills as a tracker in the Boy Scouts.

I had a wonderful time in the Scouts. In no time at all, I had been given a troop all to myself. I can still remember the sense of self-respect and accomplishment I felt when my Scoutmaster took me aside and informed me that a brand new patrol was being concocted solely to incorporate my unique personality.

'It's going to be called "The Just Jolly Patrol",' he said, smiling at me indulgently.

'Is that because it will function on a sense of justice and fair play for all, regardless of race, creed or colour, sir?' I asked, my face almost purple with pride.

'No, it's because it will be just you that is in it,' he said, jabbing a finger into my chest so that I would never forget the importance of the honour I had been awarded. Then, as if to emphasise this important award, he informed me that all my fellow Scouts had threatened to give up Scouting forever unless I was given a patrol all to myself.

I'm not afraid to admit that a tear escaped from the corner of my eye, not a tear of self-indulgent pride, more a tear of pain because, when the Scoutmaster jabbed me in the chest, he inadvertently hit me on the nipple and, it being a particularly cold day, my nipple had been rubbing against the hair shirt I had been given as a welcome present from the troop. I'll never forget that moment, not only for the sentiments that had been expressed by my fellow Scouts but also because I've had a permanent dent in my nipple ever since.

I eventually tracked Ewen Mee to a little-used private room in the east wing of the castle. Her Majesty never visited this room so we were guaranteed uninterrupted privacy. Whilst on the subject of Her Majesty (actually Her Majesty is not, of course, a subject – it's us who are the subjects – but you know what I mean), I have, surprisingly, only met her the once. That was when I first arrived. She graciously granted me an audience and urged me to tell her all about my adventures with the poor unfortunate, who was wired up to the moon, that I spoke about earlier. Apparently, she had just been through an extremely exacting day and hoped that I would give her an advertissement (I think that should be *divertissement*) to take her out of herself so she could forget her cares and relax. I replied, with a curtsy in my voice, that I was very nervous at meeting her. 'Just tell me all about it, in your own way,' she said, nodding graciously.

As I embarked on my dissertation I noticed, after a while, that her concentration level was so intense her eyes glazed over and her head nodded graciously a lot more. She then got so relaxed that she started to yawn graciously too. I knew I had succeeded in my task when she started slumping in her seat and eventually fell off it altogether. Rising graciously from the floor, she rubbed her eyes and sighed. 'That's enough. You obviously have hidden shallows that we may explore another day.' And, with another gracious yawn, she left. I made to follow but her corgis snapped protectively at my ankles, before scampering off to join their mistress.

Naturally it was one of Ephesia's ambitions to meet with Her Majesty. I believe Her Majesty was interested in meeting Ephesia too as she was heard to say that she had never met anyone who combed their hair with an egg beater. Ephesia did meet Prince Philip though. The occasion was not a total success as it was during the shooting season and he mistook her for a stag. She happened to be clearing the hallway out and was crossing the road holding a hat rack in front of her. She had also unfortunately tied a clothesline round her waist, the end of which was dragging on the ground behind her. For those of you who don't know Ephesia, I should, in the Prince's defence, point out that she, shall we say, selects from the outsize rail in the clothes shops. She did try to lose weight by going on a diet consisting only of bananas and coconuts. She didn't lose any weight but, by God, she can climb a tree. Ephesia's idea of a balanced diet is a bar of chocolate in each hand. One of the reasons for my marrying her was that I reasoned that I was getting two for the price of one – in fact, I'm still not sure if I'm in breech of the law on bigamy. She is also not blessed with an absence of facial hair. So, with a cry of 'Look at the giblets on that!', Philip fired off a salvo. Ephesia, in self-defence, went straight into attack mode and charged him. His Royal Highness, never having been in a situation where the prey attacked him, dropped his gun, ran for cover and embraced vegetarianism for six months.

By the time I arrived, the Very Reverend Mee's nose had stopped bleeding. He was sitting behind what looked like a small child's desk and sniffing tentatively to check that the flow of blood had, indeed, ceased. Strangely, he did not look out of place sitting there.

'Take eh seat, Jolly,' he said, pointing to the other side of the desk. 'There's eh cher beh thet sedboard there thet you ken dreg over.' As I positioned the chair, he continued, 'Eh'll get straight to the point. However, before Eh get to thet point, Eh must hev your essurence thet what Eh em ehbout to tell you will go no further then this room. This is of peremount importence.' He leaned forward on his chair and fixed me with a cold, hard stare that meant that what he meant meant business. 'Do Eh hev thet essurence, Jolly?'

A strange feeling swept over me and I instinctively reached for my old companion Teddy who is a small bear I rescued at a bring-and-buy sale. To celebrate my thirtieth birthday, I had thrown away my comfort blanket and adopted him as my special friend. Uneasily, I realised that, not expecting anything untoward, I had left Teddy guarding my room.

'Ehmm! Perhaps you could tell me what it is that you want to tell me and then I can tell you if I can be trusted not to tell Ephesia if she threatens to break my arm unless I tell her what I'm not supposed to,' I ventured. 'It's just that she has an uncanny knack of knowing when I'm not disclosing everything to her and she's an awful lot stronger than me, you see.'

Ewen Mee leaned back, his hands together, the left thumb resting lightly on the right thumb and all the corresponding digits doing likewise. He gently drew both hands apart, then tapped them together as he studied me intently. 'You're eh total wimp, eren't you?' he said at last.

'Not total,' I blasted back. 'If Teddy were here, you'd see a different, more confident me.'

Mee whistled silently before replying. 'Eh think you hed better fetch Teddy because Eh hev eh feeling you're going to need him.' He drew out a pipe cleaner from his top pocket and started to shove it up his right nostril. 'While you er doing thet Eh'll set about unblocking meh nose.'

All the way back to the quarters Ephesia and I had been allotted when we first arrived at Balmoral, I sensed that something momentous was again about to enter into my life. But what was it? What task did my Saviour want me to undertake? What . . . ? Actually, to clear up the matter of the living quarters, it's not strictly true to say that they were the ones we had been allotted when we first arrived. The original living arrangements were actually in the castle. After my audience with Her Majesty, however, we were allotted the present ones – well, the plural doesn't really apply as it is not so much quarters as an eighth. It was explained to me that it was a theme house that had been modelled to look like a shed. The name of the house is Base Camp One. It's half a mile away from the castle and can only be reached after an hour's strenuous climb up a high precipice which is known locally as Pariah's Peak. I must try to find out who Pariah was and also remember to thank Her Majesty for providing Ephesia and I with such a good view. Apparently, it was at her command that we were given such a prestigious place to live.

As I made my way towards Pariah's Peak, I decided that there was no point in racking my brain trying to guess the purpose that had brought Ewen Mee here. The Lord would provide the answer in his own good time and, whatever his bidding was, then I, as his loyal servant, would endeavour to carry out his wishes. The words of Isaiah 20:12:

> They shall call the nobles thereof to the kingdom but none shall be there and all her princes shall be nothing.

came to mind and I immediately felt lighter in spirit and a spring came back into my stride – I have no idea why.

I returned to the castle with Teddy in my pocket. The fading light and the drop in temperature signalled Dusk was approaching and I hailed him loudly. 'Hello, how are you this fine evening, then? Enjoying the night air?' Campbell Dusk, the Queen's head gillie, surveyed me through eyes that looked as if they had spent many a winter's night searching the horizon for game. His skin was a bright red – indeed, almost crimson in places. He had a mane of wild silver hair that framed a face that was traced with lines of wisdom – a wisdom that had been passed on from ancestors that had strode these hills and glens for centuries. As you looked into those eyes, you could imagine that long-forgotten storms had slammed into his face, battering it into the craggy features of a typical Highlander. If, however, you did imagine that, you would be totally mistaken. He was from Surbiton and had got the job because he was a friend of someone in the castle who was responsible for hiring and firing. He certainly looked the part and he was a very nice chap into the bargain.

'I say, old boy, is it me or is the night air a bit whiffy?'

'No! It's not you, Campbell,' I explained. 'Ephesia was spreading compost and it's still lingering slightly. Will we see you at church on Sunday? Haven't seen you there for a while now.'

'Spot on, old boy. I've been watching television quite a bit recently. I find it much more preferable than listening to you waffling on about some two-thousand-year-old desert prophet. Don't you know, what?'

I must admit that this left me a bit puzzled.

'Don't I know what?' I asked.

'Eh?' he asked back.

'You asked me "Don't you know what?" and I'm asking you back "Don't I know what?",' I said by way of an explanation.

Campbell Dusk shook his head and then snapped his fingers. 'Ah! I see what's gone wrong. It doesn't actually mean anything. "Don't you know, what?" is an expression used by chaps of good breeding!'

'I haven't a clue. You tell me. What is an expression used by chaps of good breeding?'

'I've told you "Don't you know, what?" is an expression used by chaps of good breeding,' he shouted, the veins on his neck starting to protrude.

'And I've told you,' my neck protruded back at his neck, 'that I don't know what is an expression used by chaps of good breeding. As a matter of fact, I am not even interested any more but I'll tell you this. There's an expression, used by folk that work in the docks where I come from, that, if I wasn't a Church of Scotland minister, I would love to tell you about. Suffice it to say, it involves placing chaps of good breeding up your sit-upon.' And, I continued, 'When you're standing in front of your creator on judgement day and you ask him if you can come into heaven, even though you'd rather watch television than attend his house, considering he can do miracles, he's liable to stick considerably more than a few chaps of good breeding up your sit-upon.' As I strode away from him, I shouted back over my shoulder. 'What do you have to say to that?'

'You've dropped your teddy bear,' he said with what I thought was a slightly mocking tone in his voice. 'Hope he hasn't hurt himself,' he continued with a smirk, walking away from me. I, of course, knew that Teddy was made of sterner stuff and that a little fall was not going to deter him from protecting me. As I lifted his little body up from the path, I noticed that Teddy had somehow picked up a large stone and, before I could say 'No, Teddy!', he had hurled it with an unerring accuracy at Campbell. It struck him firmly on the top of his thick silver mane. With a yelp, he turned round and shook his fist at us. 'You, sir, are a bounder! I have a mind to give you a good beating!' he shouted.

'Come ahead! You couldn't beat a carpet,' Teddy shouted back, sounding a bit like me, strangely. His little paws were now gesturing to Campbell, beckoning to him, urging him on. Teddy armed himself with more stones that I had picked up for him and carpet-bombed him with them. Again, they found their mark with seeming infallibility. Realising that Teddy was not for backing down, Campbell started to lose his original bravado.

'You're very brave when there are two of you, aren't you?' There was a look of fear and incomprehension in his eyes. I also noticed he was starting to back off, his whole body language was one of submission and retreat.

'I promise to stay out of it,' I offered.

'Yes! It'll be just you and me!' Teddy bellowed. I helped him to lift a strand of hay, that had been used for feeding the horses, from the ground and placed it in front of us. There was now a quiet menace in his voice. 'OK, punk, pick it up and break it in two!'

Campbell stared at Teddy as if he couldn't believe what he was seeing. Teddy returned his stare. 'What you have to decide here, punk, is how many stones do I have left. I may have a really big one that could mash your stupid red face into pulp. On the other hand, I may have used them all up. I guess the choice is yours.' The air was heavy with a menace you could almost touch. Teddy's voice was now almost a whisper. 'I guess it's make your mind up time, huh? C'mon, punk, break my hay.'

This seemed to be the straw (or hay) that broke the camel's (or Campbell's) back because he ran off, holding his head and screaming. I looked at Teddy and knew I had to ask, 'Did you have one more stone, Teddy?'

Still staring at the fast-fading Dusk, he said, without looking round, 'That's an answer you'll never know, preacher.'

Teddy's quiet courage seemed to fortify me for my meeting with Ewen Mee. Whatever it was he had to tell me, I was now ready for it. But what could it be? As I made my way to what I now know was my date with destiny, I munched thoughtfully on a slice of bread which had been spread with some dock leaf and nettle jam that Ephesia had kindly left for me in the fridge – or, to call it by it's other name, the dining room. The dock and nettle jam was one of Ephesia's own concoctions. It was a very clever and well-thought-out recipe. Though the nettle jam stung your mouth viciously the dock leaf simultaneously kept the swelling down to a minimum. She is very adventurous in the kitchen (or would be if we had a kitchen) and is working feverishly on her next project – wasp and calamine piccalilli.

19

The initial swelling in my mouth was just fading away as I knocked on the door of the room I had left Ewen Mee in. 'Is thet you, Jolly?' Mee's voice responded from behind the door.

'Yes. It's me, Mee,' I echoed back. 'Teddy's here as well.'

There was a noise, for all the world, like a sigh of dismay before Mee spoke again. 'Come in, both of you.' Mee was lying on the floor with his head held back and a spoon jutting out from behind his neck.

'Has the bleeding not stopped, then?' I enquired needlessly.

'Almost,' he replied, trying not to speak through his nose. 'Eh'm efraid Eh did more demage then good with the pep cleaner. Eh must hev shoved it up too fer, hit something vital and then pessed out. Eh came round about ten minutes ego.' He surveyed us both from his position on the floor. 'Hev eh seat. Does emmm Teddy need eh seat too? He ken hev mehn es Eh'm not using it et the moment.'

'Och, No! He'll be fine sitting on my knee,' I explained as I sat down on the chair. Teddy perched himself on my knee and gave my hand a reassuring squeeze with both his paws. 'Now, then, what is this all about?' I asked, leaning over and adjusting the spoon that was sticking out from his back.

'Eh told you – Eh fainted due to shoving eh pep cleaner too far up meh nostril.'

'No, not that,' I said, not wanting to get into another bout of misunderstanding. 'Why have you come all the way from Church of Scotland headquarters to see me? You sounded as if it was very important.'

'How reht you ehr, Jolly. It is important. In fect, it could be vhettel.'

A low whistle escaped from Teddy's lips as he looked up at me. 'I think you had better explain what you want from him or me,' Teddy or I said.

Ewen Mee rose gingerly from his prone position and, equally gingerly, settled into his chair behind the aforementioned desk.

'Eh say, Jolly, do you think we could conduct this meeting without your little pel? It's very disconcerting trehing to hev eh conversation with both you end Rupert.'

'Teddy!' I corrected him quickly enough to stop Teddy going berserk (or bearserk). 'I wouldn't call him Rupert if I were you. Believe me, you don't want to get him angry.' Curiously, Ewen Mee gave me a similar look to that given me by Campbell Dusk.

'Uh-huh!' he said in a long drawn-out, beginning-to-see-the-light sort of way. 'Eh'm not suggesting thet we do ehway with – emmm – Teddy. No, no! Eh'm merely esking if you could place him somewhere thet he meht not be queht so prominent, perheps. Do you get meh drift?'

I was loath to ask Teddy if this would be all right as he had come all this way with me but I needn't have worried. Without me even looking at him, he realised what was required of him, got off my knee and snuggled up inside my jacket.

'Thenk you, Teddy,' the Very Reverend Ewen Mee acknowledged. Teddy's head popped out from my jacket and gave him the thumbs up.

A few seconds later, a gentle snoring from behind the breast pocket of my jacket informed me that he was fast asleep. 'He won't waken up for a long time. You can talk in complete confidence now. So, tell me, what is all this and how does it affect me?'

'Eh'll enswer the first pert of your question first. Es usual the church's stending within socehty could do with a bit of improvement. Congregations ehr still getting smaller end it's becoming, not to put too fen eh point on it, eh losing behttle. Anyhoo! The great end the good got together to treh to solve what is fest becoming eh perennial problem end they decehded, in their wisdom, thet what was needed was something called the feel-good fector. Now don't esk me what thet is. Ehs eh long-serving Church of Scotlend minister, Eh'm not au fait.' He paused to see that I was taking everything in. 'You understand?'

'Not quite,' I replied. 'You're not awffy what?'

His face again registered puzzlement, then recognition flashed across his face. 'You hev the wrong end of the stick, Jolly. *Au fait* is French it means "not familiar", "not well versed".'

'Is that right?' I decided just to go along with him. He could hardly speak English, never mind French, but sometimes it's better to keep schtumm, which, by the way, is German.

'Ehbout two weeks ego, eh summit was held to desed how to teckle this problem or, es the Moderator leks to call it, "oor wee stushie".' He broke into a fit of smirking at this. 'He is en unconscious comedien, he really is. Every time he comes out with thet phrase everyone collepses in convivielity.'

I felt it appropriate to join in. 'It must make you all feel wonderfully gay.'

'Well, Eh wouldn't go thet fer, Jolly, but it does relex us et moments of despair and heh tension. Which brings me beck to you. The Moderator was mendful of your lest exploits end the heh profile thet the church enjoyed for a wee whale. So with . . .'

'Excuse me, Reverend Mee, what wee whale?' I asked. 'I don't remember being involved with a wee whale. You're perhaps confusing me with Jonah. Mind you, that was quite a big whale.'

'Whale? Jonah? What on erth er you on about, mehn?'

'You were talking about the church's high profile and how it had enjoyed it for a wee whale.'

'Eh never mentioned any whale. Eh said thet we hed enjoyed eh heh profile temporerily – thet is to say, for eh wee whale.'

Scratching my head, I pondered this. I definitely did not remember any whale small or large. The Very Reverend Mee was obviously in some kind of hallucinogenic state because he was pondering too. Perhaps he had lost too much blood with the nosebleed.

I decided to just play along. 'Oh, THAT wee whale. I

remember it now,' I said, turning away so he would not detect that I wasn't being entirely truthful with him.

'Good. Well, Eh'm gled we cleared thet up.' He studied me intently for a second or two. 'It is cleared up? Yes? Eh hev your word on thet?'

'Oh, yes,' I lied. 'It was a very nice wee whale. I remember it well.'

Mee looked at me. I could tell his mind was still in pondering mode because he had absent-mindedly poked half his pinky finger up his right nostril thereby causing his right eye to cross ever so slightly towards his left eye.

'You know there er times, Jolly, when Eh wonder if you're on the same plenit es the rest of us. If Eh may, Eh will continue with what brought me here. Es Eh explained before,' he said, removing his pinky from his nostril and thereby, at a stroke, restoring the equilibrium to his features. 'We hev to fend some way to boost ettendences end, of course, eh bit of positive publicity will hopefully lead to thet heppy state of effairs. End thet is where your name was brought up. It was egreed thet, if we could find some suitable – shell we say – exploit thet you could become involved or entegled with, then the resultent publicity would hopefully follow. Thet is if you were egreeable? Eh must stress here, Jolly, thet we, es eh body, would not want you to do anything egainst your better judgement even although eh negative response from you could, in theory, scupper any chence of promotion. Before Eh go any further, Eh must know if you would be willing to perticipate in the scheme es presented so fer. Eh must also tell you thet the ectual proposition is still eh mystery to me end is in en envelope locked in eh vault et the benk. Eh believe, however, thet it is of moderate risk but could, in theory, make you famous end eh lot of money.'

'You mean I could be a rich pastor?'

'Possibly, should you eccept the chellenge. Of course, es eh mehn of the cloth, the only reason you should consider this

23

proposition is not for the fame end untold wealth thet may ensue but for the setisfection of knowing thet you hev served your church. You do egree?'

'Absolutely,' I enthused. 'When would I get the money?'

'First things first.' Reaching into his inside jacket pocket, he drew out a folded sheet of paper. 'Eh must now formally esk you to sign this document which ebsolves the Church from any claim thet meht erise from this leap into the unknown – hereinefter known as "the venture" –' he flattened out the document on the desk, 'end commits you to the venture even though you hev no idea what the venture is end even though the venture could result in you – hereinefter known es the "venturer" – becoming known hereinefter es the deceased should the demise of the venturer-stroke-deceased lead him to the spirit world – hereinefter known es the "here-efter". If you would lek to segn et the bottom there where it says "segn et the bottom here", we ken proceed with the next stage.'

'Would that mean I could get the money quicker?'

He glanced up at me sharply.

'Thus enabling me to serve the church and solve the Moderator's "wee stushie",' I added, quick as a flash with a roguish smirk, which made Ewen Mee smirk as well.

'Oh, Eh'm forgetting – perheps you should talk this over with your good lady. You must remember thet you meht hev to be ehway from her for some considerable period of tehm. Thet may hev to be taken into eccount before you fenally segn.'

'You're right. Where do I sign again?'

He pointed to the bottom of the contract. As I put pen to the paper, he continued talking. 'Eh'll bring the envelope on Seturday. Eh believe the Heghland Games er on et Braemer. If you could errange to be there, Eh'll orgenise the constebulary to hev eh special prevate tent made eveilable. Ken you do thet?'

'No problem,' I replied, handing him the document. 'I was going in my capacity of minister anyway. Also, Ephesia is defending her status as last year's shot-putt, caber-tossing, hammer-throwing champion and, of course, she is captain of the tug-of-wart team.'

'You mean "war", of course,' he interjected.

'No,' I replied, leaving it there.

'Hes she given up on the cetch-es-cetch-ken wrestling, then?' Ewen Mee asked, sounding surprised. Obviously Ephesia's fame as a grappler had spread all the way to Edinburgh.

'Not exactly given up,' I answered. 'She was asked not to compete as she always won and the other wrestlers complained she was too rough.'

Ewen Mee jumped down from his seat behind the desk and offered his hand. 'Till Seterday, then? Ehnd, Eh need herdly edd, not eh word to anyone on this metter.'

'Trust me on that.' We shook hands and left the room to go our separate ways – he to Edinburgh and I to serve my Church selflessly. If untold adventures, separation from Ephesia and pots of money were the by-products of that, well, I would just have to grit my teeth and accept it.

As I approached Base Camp One there was a pungent odour of dead leaves, old wood and damp twigs being burned – a sure sign that Ephesia was at home and dinner was being prepared. She had just finished a woodland and self-sufficiency course and was practising living off the land. I was obliged to practise along with her or life would not have been worth living. I was reminded of Exodus 3:2:

> Behold, the bush burned with fire and the bush was not consumed

How true. Except, of course, in my case, it would be consumed – by me.

She really was a wizard of the culinary arts and one of the many health benefits I derived from her adventurous cooking was a capacity to swallow just about anything without actually vomiting. Once I visited the doctor for a check up and, after examining my blood, he was amazed by my capacity to fight off infection. Apparently my white corpuscles have fought off so many infections, due to my eating Ephesia's food, that they are now in a state of constant readiness. The doctor explained this to me by comparing my white corpuscles to the ordinary person's. 'Yours are like the Special Air Services, everyone else's are like the Special Needs Services.'

I bought her a cookbook for her Christmas but she never used it. I asked her why and she said it was too demanding, explaining that all the recipes began the same way – 'Take a clean dish.'

We had the royal gardener and his wife round for dinner and Ephesia burnt some venison steaks especially for them. After his first bite there was a puzzled look on his face and he asked, 'What is this? Is it pork?'

'No,' responded Ephesia, a smile playing at the edges of her lips.

'Is it some kind of mutant chicken?' his wife asked, prodding at it with her fork.

'I'll give you a clue,' Ephesia said. 'It's what you may think I probably call my husband.'

'Oh, I've never tasted windbag before,' said the gardener.

I said nothing. However, I'd bet anything that my corpuscles would give his corpuscles a doing any day.

'Hello, cupcake, I'm home,' I coughed, as the smoke from dinner engulfed me at the front door. 'What's for dinner?'

My dear wife was bent double over a large cooking pot that was bubbling away in the open hearth. She was shovelling ingredients into this pot with a large shovel that we kept for that purpose and then, after stirring them with a garden fork, she tasted the concoction with the aid of a smaller shovel that we kept for tasting.

She lifted her head up to greet me – her dear face blackened from the smoke. There was some indistinguishable form of boiled vegetable dripping down each side of her mouth because the shovel had proved too wide to fit even Ephesia's gaping maws. She handed me a toadstool.

'I found these mushrooms in a clearing under a rotting tree. I'm not sure if they're poisonous. Try one for me.' I, of course, was only too happy to oblige. The usual method was that I would bite into the raw mushroom and see if my teeth began to tingle and my gums recede. If this didn't happen, then it was on to stage two – swallowing the mushroom. Then, if I didn't have to rush for the outside loo five minutes after swallowing it, it was presumed safe to cook the fungi. But, even if it proved to be not fit for normal consumption – remember our corpuscles were the crème de la crème – Ephesia wasted nothing. She would sell what was left to the castle staff as a diuretic-come-weight-loss potion. On this occasion, there was nothing to fear – indeed, it proved to be a very tasty toadstool.

I decided not to mention Ewen Mee's proposed adventure as I had been put on trust and had given my word of honour. Also, Ephesia could have turned violent if she thought I was going to enjoy myself without her permission.

'Can I help?' I offered – knowing the offer would be declined. Ephesia informed me that we were having leftovers. This was usual. We always had leftovers – in fact, we've had leftovers so many times, we now can't remember the original meal.

She carried over a plateful of steaming vegetation. I could discern some pinecones, some coarse grasses, bits of old tree bark, some indistinct form of roots and a long-abandoned bird's nest. She returned to the table with a bowl of thin watery soup alongside a small plate of something that was still smouldering.

'What's the soup, dear?' I asked. She liked me to do this so she could surprise me with what she had rustled up out of the blue.

'It's new. I call it thin water soup with a flambé of wild woodland worms. Actually the worms caught fire and the soup is what I put the flames out with.' Again I could only marvel at her ability to turn disaster into triumph. 'Dig in,' she said. 'I had to – the worms were hiding from me again.'

As I set about clearing my plates, my mind turned to the meeting I had just had with the Very Reverend Ewen Mee. Usually I cannot wait for Sunday to come round and my mind is full of thoughts of what the theme of my sermon will be, how the congregation will find it and, indeed, how they will find the church – it's been so long since most of them actually turned up. However, this time, I could not wait for Saturday.

Ephesia sensed something. Without looking up, I sensed that she sensed something. 'Looking forward to Saturday and defending all your titles at the Braemar Games, dear?' I asked, evasively, while picking a bit of burnt worm from my teeth with a thorn from a leftover hawthorn branch. 'Is there any more soup? It was delicious.' Turning the tap on, she poured me another bowl of thin water soup and put it down in front of my table.

'There you are,' she said. 'You've had the last of the burnt worms. Do you want pudding?'

'Not unless you've made something special, cherub – I'm actually quite full.' I patted my tum-tum to emphasise this. 'Mmmmmmm! That was good.'

'The pudding is quite like the soup. It's cream of burnt worm sauce, poured over a terrine of sticky willies and battered beetles.' There was a faint, almost undetectable, air of menace in her tone that I picked up on, informing me I should consider the pudding in a favourable light.

'Well, I am absolutely packed, petal.' I saw a hackle imperceptibly rise. 'But,' I wheedled, 'how can I resist battered beetles and cream of burnt worm sauce?' Easily, was, of course, the answer to that one but it would have taken a more resolute spirit than I was given, to have chanced replying in the negative. The lone hackle fell back in place and I knew I was on safe ground again.

Pudding was duly got through and, after some initial retching, I sat back and once more breached the question of her attendance at the Braemar Games. I had to find out what contests she was going to attend. As a loving spouse, it was my duty to cheer her on and it was also my duty, as the minister, to show support to the defeated male contestants and tell them not to feel too bad at being horsed, once again, by a woman. I always found that a pat on the back and a cheery bit of encouragement to keep on trying even newer performance-enhancing drugs seem to buck them up.

I have to admit that, even though pride is a sin, I am secretly pleased at how Ephesia has helped the pharmaceutical companies try out their latest concoctions on the contestants in a valiant effort to try to beat her. They are illegal but the authorities turn a blind eye. If they didn't, Ephesia would turn it into a black eye. It was also imperative for me to know when I could sneak away and find out what grand plan the church had in store for me.

'Oh, I'm just going in for the usual stuff. Frankly, I'm getting a bit bored at the lack of competition in the strength events,' she simpered with a virile growl. 'Maybe I should enter for the Highland dancing again. I felt last year that I didn't really do myself justice.'

My mind recalled and then recoiled at the memory of everyone running for cover at what they thought was a rumble of thunder but turned out to be Ephesia limbering up by practising her, for want of a better word, dance steps – the swords bouncing around the stage uncontrollably when her size thirteens thudded on to the rostrum during the sword dance, one of the swords skewering a judge (subsequently retired), then the stage finally giving up the ghost and collapsing during the Highland fling.

'I know it was only my first time and I didn't really expect to win,' she mused, 'but I think I deserved at least a placing, don't you?'

'I certainly do, dumpling.' (I feel white lies are sometimes justified.)

'I think it may have been because I don't come from the Highlands and they are biased against me. What do you think?' she said, a trifle peevishly.

'You may very well have hit the nail on the head, precious,' I replied, judiciously. Ephesia nodded in agreement, wistfully releasing my arm from around my back.

'Shall we sit outside for a while and take in the air and the view, princess?' I said, relief in my voice that white-lie time was over, at least for the moment. As we sat there, gazing out from Pariah's Peak, far from the hurly-burly of modern life with all its stresses and strains, its injustices and tales of woe, I reflected how Shakespeare had put it so well in Hamlet's oration to Othello.

Shall I compare thee to a lump of clay?
Nay, thou art more lumpier and more clayier.

Eh! I think I may have got that wrong. It couldn't have been Hamlet because Hamlet is, of course, a cigar. Come to think of it, I'm not even sure if it was Shakespeare. I have a feeling it might have been the Greek philosopher Harry Stopheles. Whoever it was, they undoubtedly captured the moment for me as Ephesia and I sat there. She at one edge of the precipice, me at the other more perilous bit, letting the ambience of our relationship settle in around us.

Some folks will never know what it means to come home to a little affection, a little tenderness and even a little sympathy and understanding. I'm lucky enough to know what it means – it means I'm in the wrong house.

❖   ❖   ❖

The day of my destiny had finally arrived. I had found it very difficult to sleep last night. Not only due to the excitement of what was lying in store for me but also because there had been a storm during the night. When morning eventually arrived, Ephesia and I had an argument and she hasn't spoken to me since. It started when I asked Ephesia if she had heard the storm during the night. 'No,' she said, irritably. 'Was there thunder as well?' I nodded my head sleepily, in affirmation. 'Why didn't you wake me?' she rounded on me, abrasively. 'You know I can never sleep when it thunders.'

I left her searching for her Highland-dancing shoes. I believe they are called 'Predators' and are recommended by David Beckham. With her it's not so much *Bend It Like Beckham* as *Eviscerate It Like Ephesia*.

I actually found myself whistling cheerfully as I approached the bus stop that would take me to Braemar and to my appointment with destiny. As I stood waiting for the local bus, a spot of rain landed up my nose. You may well wonder why I say 'up' rather than 'on' my nose. The reason was, quite simply, I happened to be looking towards the sky to check if I had felt a spot of rain on my head – in which case, I would have known that I had forgotten my hat. Thus, with my nose pointed skywards, the spot of rain went up rather than on my nose. I just wanted to clear that up. As it happened, I had no time to go back and get my hat because the bus to Braemar appeared just then and, as there wasn't another one for an hour and a half, I decided I might as well go for it and brave the elements without my headgear.

As the bus pulled up, I could see that the driver was a great old character called Angus MacAroni. Although originally of Italian extraction, he was fiercely proud of his Highland heritage. Indeed, his father had changed the spelling of their last name to make it sound more Scottish. Angus carried on that tradition by insisting on the Highland pronunciation of his first name – this being 'Oienghoos'. Although he insisted on being called by the Highland pronunciation, nobody actually did so as it was a hellish thing to get your tongue round. Indeed, wee Mrs Ivy Rae lost a perfectly good upper set of false teeth trying, not only dutifully but also verbally, to negotiate her way round his first name. However, the fact that nobody ever called him what he wanted them to call him led to him having a somewhat surly disposition. Of course, I always felt that he had a wee soft spot for me as I at least always attempted to pronounce his name correctly.

Stepping on board the bus, I noticed that there was quite a few passengers. 'I see you have quite a load on, Oy-Eh! Ogy-Oyeginyoos,' I remarked, doffing my hat to the ladies and immediately feeling a bit foolish because, of course, I had forgotten to put it on.

'I haven't touched a drop,' he snapped back, surveying me with what, for all the world, looked like grim hostility but was probably not.

'Well, I am sorry if I offended you but, I assure you, if I did, it was not meant, Ogynoo-Oyagannny-emm! Oh-ay Aa-Agnus.'

The front passengers, two little boys, started to snigger and then laugh out loud. 'Hey, driver, he called you Agnes!'

'I did not,' I said, back in white-lie territory, fixing the two of them with what I hoped was a stern gaze.

'It sounded like "Agnes" to me,' said Agnes.

'What made you think I said "Agnes"?' I replied, keeping my eye on the two miscreants.

'Because that's my name.'

I turned round and realised that I was talking to a rather florid-looking woman who was perched on the edge of her seat, balancing a bird cage, with some indeterminate bird inside it, on her knee. I say 'indeterminate' because there was a cloth hanging over the cage, thus obscuring the view of what was actually inside. 'You definitely said "Agnes". I've heard it enough in my lifetime to know it when I hear it,' she continued, unhelpfully.

Angus pulled hard on his brake. He didn't move but said through clenched teeth, 'Don't you ever call me "Agnes" again.' I realised that things were getting out of hand. I also realised I didn't have Teddy to help – which made me panic slightly.

'I can assure you Agne-, I mean Angu-, I mean An-, Ann- . . .'

'Hey, driver, he just called you "Anne",' piped up the slightly larger of the two boys. His little friend held up two thumbs to him and they both sat gleefully watching the panic that was now starting to well up within me.

Angus sat holding his steering wheel tightly, his knuckles white and cracking as if under strain. I felt, if I could just get him to listen to my side of the misunderstanding, all would be well.

'Eh! Ah!' I was finding it very difficult to control my thoughts as everyone was staring at me. Now, then, I thought, just get him to listen – that was the key to calming things down. I began again, 'Eh! Ah! . . . Just . . . Ah! . . . Ah! . . . List . . .'

Before I could finish, the bigger of the two delinquents again piped up, 'Hey, driver, he's calling you "Alice" noo!' His evil little friend slapped him on the back and they both sat back in their seats, chortling and smothering their laughter with one hand while pointing at me with the other.

Angus still hadn't turned round but there was a nervous energy coming from him that you could almost touch. His voice cut through the eerie silence that had descended on the by now enthralled passengers.

'Say one more word and I warn you, man of the cloth or no man of the cloth, I will tear you limb from limb.' Fortunately for me I was at a loss for words.

'Piss off, Agnes,' I heard myself say in a disembodied voice.

A gasp rose from every seat.

'What did you say?' Angus released one hand from the steering wheel at the same time as everyone else got out of their seats and moved to the back of the bus – there to crouch in anticipation.

'Piss off, Agnes.' There it was again.

'Hey, driver, he told you to piss off,' said you-know-who, rather needlessly.

As I glanced round, hoping for some form of assistance from my fellow cowards, I noticed that the cloth had fallen away from the birdcage, displaying therein a large and exceedingly ugly bird belonging to some branch of the parrot family.

'Piss off, Agnes,' it said in an almost perfect replication of my voice.

As Angus turned round to distribute vigilante justice to yours truly, I pointed at the bird. 'It wasn't me, Ang-Angnug . . . It was him,' I said, pointing at the bird.

'Indeed, it was not. My Polly wouldn't use that language,' barked Agnes, the florid female who was frantically trying to replace the cover over the parrot.

'Piss off, Agnes,' croaked Polly for the entire bus to hear. All their attention was now on the Bird Woman of Braemar. Florid Features' eyes flitted round the bus before alighting on mine. 'Eh! Right, I admit it. I'm on my way in to the vet with him.' She shook the cage vigorously. 'Piss off, Agnes,' was the not altogether unexpected retort from within the cage.

'I've had enough,' Agnes rasped. 'He was my husband's bird. I gave the best years o' my life to that man but we quarrelled continuously. It wasn't my fault. Just because I wouldn't let him smoke or go out for a drink to that vile and sinful public house or let him waste his time watching shinty and going to the bookmakers. Then, the last straw was when he asked if he could have a television in the house so he could watch sport. I, of course, put my foot down and said no.

"However," I said, "if you're so bored, I'll tell you what I am willing to do to brighten up your days and nights." ' Here, she paused for maximum effect, ' "I'll let you sit in the big room and hold my knitting for me. It's that or nothing. What's your answer?" '

'Piss off, Agnes,' squawked Polly bang on cue.

'He went out and never came back. I got a letter from him yesterday, saying he'd found another bird and would not be back for this creature here. I've been left with him. He embarrasses me constantly so I'm having him put down.'

Cries of 'Oh! Shame! Give him another chance!' came from all round the bus.

'No, I'm not having him use language in my house,' she said, shaking her head vehemently.

'Show a bit of mercy, Agnes,' I pleaded. 'He's one of God's creatures – an innocent who has no idea what he's saying. Why not open your heart and let him in?' I said with a gentle edge to my voice.

'You open yours and let him in,' she grated back.

The rest of the passengers joined in and urged me to open my heart to Polly. This threw me somewhat and, in my own defence, I did consider it but, reluctantly, I explained that, as a minister in the Church of Scotland, it could be very compromising for me to have a parrot that used language in the house. I assured them all that, if it wasn't for the language, I would have been proud to take Polly. Secretly, I worried what Ephesia's or, indeed, Teddy's reaction to sharing me with some other creature would be.

'Please, Minister,' said one of the two runts in the front seat ominously, 'I know how you can cure Polly from using bad language. My daddy cured our parrot when it started to swear.' At least he's trying to be constructive, I thought. However, if he was right and could cure the bird from using inappropriate language, I might get landed with it. I was in a bit of a cleft palate situation. I also didn't trust the little beggars.

'How did he manage that?' I enquired, a note of scepticism in my voice letting him know I wasn't on the hook, so to speak.

'Please, Minister, I–I . . .,' his voice trailed away and he looked nervously around him. Although he was the larger of the two, he was now the centre of our attention and he was obviously ill at ease. He shifted nervously in his seat.

'Well?' I urged.

He sank into the back of the seat, all confidence gone, and whispered something to his pal. His pal whispered back into his ear and then the parrot doctor shook his head. 'What is the matter?' I enquired.

'He doesn't want to say because he feels nervous, Minister – you being a man of God and everybody else looking at him. He's a big fearty, so he is, Minister.'

His pal punched him on the side of his arm. 'I am not a fearty,' he said, huffily.

'You are so,' his confederate squealed back, kicking him on the ankle.

'I am not.'

'You are sot.'

'Am not.'

This could have gone on for half an hour, I sensed. 'Right that's enough,' I shouted, taking control of the situation. 'Tell us how your dad cured the parrot from swearing and I'll give you ten pence each. Okay?' They looked at me as if they couldn't believe their ears. I realised I had gone over the top a bit but desperate situations call for desperate measures, as they say. I would explain later to Ephesia about the missing twenty pence. 'Hurry up now or the offer will be withdrawn.'

Greed had unfortunately triumphed over shyness for the larger one embarked on the cure straight away. 'Well,' he began, 'our parrot was all right, as far as swearing and bad-mouthing people went, until we went on holiday and left the parrot with a local home for ex-sailors.' Murmurs of disquiet floated round the bus. 'When we got back, my daddy collected him from the home and brought him back to our house. That's when we first heard him saying bad words like . . .'

'Don't repeat them,' I interjected.

'But how will you know what the words were unless I say them?'

'Minister, there were words like "ba . . .".'

I was in like a flash. 'It's not necessary for me to hear them – I can imagine.' A murmur of shock went round the bus. 'I once had a parish in Glasgow,' I explained. A murmur of understanding followed the murmur of shock.

'Shall I go on, Minister?' asked the boy with a new look of respect in his eyes.

'Yes, please do, son.'

'Well, we didn't know what to do either and then my daddy read in this book that, if you want to train animals, you should do it by using a reward system. If, for example, the animal does something wrong, something you don't want it to do, you give it a punishment, something it doesn't like.' A murmur of agreement went round the bus. The lad seemed to be gaining confidence because he was wrapped up in his explanation. He continued with the full attention of the bus. 'If, on the other hand, the animal does something you want it to do, you give it a reward, something it likes.'

'Like the twenty pence I'm shelling out to you two, eh?' I half joked. Again they looked at me with disbelief, as did the rest of the bus.

'Anyway,' he continued, 'my daddy thought that, as parrots come from hot countries, they wouldn't like the cold so, the first time our parrot swore, he grabbed it and put it in the freezer for half an hour.'

'Did it work?' I asked, my voice alive with curiosity and apprehension.

'Yes, Minister. When the parrot came out, it said, "Okay, I've learned my lesson I won't swear again but, tell me, what was the turkey in for?".'

Of course, we all had a good laugh – none more so than me. The whole bus knew we had been taken for a right load of wallies by two wee tykes. And even Agnes and Oienghoos had to smile. It all ended well. Polly found a home with someone on the bus who said they could do with the company. We all felt we had learned something by having our pomposity pricked by two wee laddies. The two boys learned a valuable lesson too. They both learned never to play a trick on a busload of adults when there's still eight miles to go till you're home and you're turfed off the bus. I'm sure they both deliberated on this after they had finished blaming each other. I also hope their wee feet weren't too sore because we confiscated their wee shoes.

As it says in the bible, 'Suffer little children?' Oh, and I saved twenty pence.

I was starting to feel a bit chilly as I stood on the wet grass outside the purvey tent. It was absolutely chucking it down. However, I couldn't get inside because the tent was full up with people also sheltering from the inclemency of the weather. I was nursing a cup of very watery tea and a quite disgusting stale and also soggy jam scone when I heard the Very Reverend Mee's voice call out, 'Jolly! There you er!' As he drew level, his voice lowered to a confidential whisper. 'Eh hev eh tent set essed for us. Er you still desehrous of taking pert in this exploit? Because Eh warn you, once insehd thet tent, there will be no going beck.' He gave me a stare of such intensity that I admit to feeling a little trepidation. Steeling myself, I nodded that I was still up for it (as the young people say). 'Very well, then, follow me.'

I followed Mee between various tents and marquees, in and

out of puddles and grass, that had been flattened with the rain and excessive trampling of Wellington boots and Land-Rover tyres, till it was like wading in an impassable muddy swamp. My feet were getting very damp and I was feeling very un-comfortable – in fact, I was just about to call the whole thing off when we came to a policeman standing outside a canvas structure with a sign above it saying 'VIP's ONLY'.

'In here,' the Very Reverend Mee gestured. When Mee showed the policeman some kind of pass, he nodded in acquies-cence and we were in. I was not prepared for what met my gaze inside. Ringing the walls of the, for want of a better word, tent, was a structure that looked like it was metallic or some such like material. This same material covered the top of the tent as well. It dawned on me that I could no longer hear the noises from outside. Even the rattle of the rain, that must still have been battering the tent, was no longer audible – unlike the jam scone which was no longer edible. Whatever I was going to be told, it was obviously not meant to be heard outside of our current surroundings.

In the middle of the space there was a table and seated at the table were three people. My heart leaped as I recognised someone I had only seen in photographs in various Church of Scotland magazines – a tall man with finely chiselled features and an easy and confident bearing that supported his well-cut Salvation Army suit. Even now, I am not allowed, for security reasons, to mention his real name. Let us, for the sake of the story, call him Major Day. Seated alongside him was a small woman who, in contrast to Day, I have to say, looked exceedingly ordinary – indeed, even nondescript. The sort of woman who always seems to hold you up at the supermarket pay desk because she wants to pay for a packet of crisps with a cheque, if you know what I mean. She had an indefinable air of abstraction about her and was in her late fifties, perhaps. You will find out her name in due course as my tale unravels.

Across the table from them was a chap of oriental extraction. He was not much bigger than Reverend Mee and was surveying me intently (no pun intended). His eyes were black as ivory and seemed to be hiding from me under the hooded eyelids. His body appeared to be encased in a black shiny full-length coat, the bottom of which trailed on the ground beneath his chair. I would have judged him to be not more than forty-something.

Both of the men rose as we approached the table, which was replete with coffee-pots and teapots, sandwiches and bottles of pure fresh water that the labels informed us came straight from a Highland stream. I made a mental note not to drink that as I had seen sheep and shepherds use these streams for all sorts of bodily functions. Major Day smiled broadly as he addressed me, 'At last, the man himself.' With the palms facing upwards, he spread out his hands. 'Ecce Homo.'

I assumed this was some sort of traditional greeting. It sounded Welsh to me although I couldn't see why a Welshman would be involved with the Church of Scotland – anyway, in for a pound, as the saying goes. I took his hand and, remembering to grasp it firmly so as not to appear weak, I greeted him in his native language. 'Eh! Yes. And may I wish you Ecce Homo too?'

A puzzled look swept over his face. (Why does everybody look puzzled when I talk to them?) 'I'm sorry?' he said, enquiringly.

I decided to speak slower as he was obviously having difficulties with the language. 'Me,' I placed both hands on my chest to let him know what me meant. 'Me would,' I knocked on the table. 'Wood, you understand? Wood? Like,' I smacked my lips, 'Like – yes? To,' I held up two fingers, 'To – yes? Wish – wish?' I crossed both my fingers, 'You,' pointing at him, 'Ecce Homo.'

The Major still looked perplexed. Ewen Mee piped in with,

'Eh'm efraid, Major Day, thet Jolly doesn't speak Letin.'

'Letin?' I queried. 'Where's that? I've never heard of Let. Is it in Wales?'

'He means Latin,' said Major Day. 'Ecce Homo is Latin for "Behold the man". I was greeting you in Latin.'

'I'm afraid you'll have to confine yourself to English,' I answered, perhaps a trifle testily. 'Latin is not exactly required reading in the Church of Scotland, you know.'

'May Eh introduce you to Major Day. He is the chep who basicelly dreamed up this venture. He is the Moderator's number one edviser.' Now, kissing his feet may seem, to some, like overdoing an apology. However, I had never met someone who had actually met the Moderator before so I think maybe the occasion got to me somewhat.

Anyway, after I had wiped the mud from his shoes off my mouth, I was introduced to the other two. Leading me over to the unprepossessing woman I described earlier, Ewen Mee introduced us. 'Reverend Jolly, may Eh introduce you to Miss Wonterland. Miss Wonterland, this is the Reverend Eh EhM Jolly.'

'I am very pleased to meet you, Miss Wonterland,' I said, bending down to take her hand. 'What an unusual name. I don't think I've come across it before in my travels.'

'Excuse me no' getting up, Reverend, but I'm a martyr tae my feet. This wet weather knocks the stuffin' oot them, so it does. I'm pleased to meet you. I'm from Glasgow, of course, as you can probably tell from the accent, but originally the family came over from Holland, that's where the name Wonterland comes in. But drop the formality and just call me Allyson.'

'Perheps Eh should tell you, Jolly, thet Miss Wonterland is erguably THE top mesmerist end teacup reader in the lend. She's played the Pevilion Theatre on more then one occasion,' Ewen Mee informed me with an ill-disguised tone of reverence in his voice. He smiled ingratiatingly at Miss Wonterland who

41

grimaced back and proceeded to rub the soles of her feet.

Turning to the oriental-looking gentleman, Mee continued with the introductions. 'End now may Eh present Doctor Hes Kmee Hwy, Tibet's foremost expert in metaphysics, who has graciously agreed to join us for our little project. So, Jolly, we hev eh cosmopoliten flavour.'

'Just plain vanilla for me, thank you,' I replied. 'I'm pleased to meet you, Doctor Has.' (I congratulated myself on having known that Mee meant Has not Hes.)

He shook his head, 'Hwy.'

I was, frankly, taken aback by his frankness, 'I just am, Doctor Has.'

'No. Hwy.'

A puzzled look swept over my face (just for a change). 'Well, to be honest, I don't really know. It's just a convention we have in this country. We just say things without really meaning them. I must say though that I admire your desire to go deeper and find the true meaning of . . .'

Major Day interrupted me, 'I think what the Doctor is trying to convey is that his name is Has Kmee Hwy, He is, therefore, called by his last name – i.e., Doctor Hwy.'

'Oh! Right.' The penny dropped and I had to smile. 'OK, Hwy.' I nodded in affirmation to the doctor.

'No!' he replied. 'Not OK Hwy – it's Has Kmee Hwy.'

'Thet's enough,' Ewen Mee shouted. 'Ken we get on with wheh we erh here?' He pointed to an empty chair positioned by itself, facing the other four chairs. 'If you would kehndly sit there, Jolly, we'll proceed.' He sat down on the fourth chair, which meant that I would be facing the four of them. As I sat down I was reminded of a probation panel I once attended. I half expected to be called the accused.

'I don't want you to feel as if you are on trial here, Jolly,' began Major Day. 'We are convinced you're the only man for the job and, anyway, there is no going back for any of us now.

So, in short,' he paused and looked around the table, 'we're stuck with each other. *Domine deus miserere nobis* which, of course, means "Lord have mercy on us". I hope you'll forgive my quoting in Latin again, Rev. Jolly,' he said with a wry smile. 'But it seems appropriate.'

I nodded and smiled wryly back so he wouldn't realise I had no idea what he was talking about.

'Your head must be bursting with a thousand questions. Now it's time to answer those questions.'

'Could you do it in English?' I ventured. Everyone laughed as though I had made a joke so I laughed as if I had made a joke as well.

'Do my best,' chuckled Major Day. 'OK, in time-honoured fashion, I'll begin at the beginning. As you are aware, the Church of Scotland, along with Churches of all denominations, is finding that our congregations are getting smaller and smaller. They are dropping at a dangerously rapid rate. There was a brief upswing to this depressing tendency last year due to your exploits, Jolly.' He nodded in my direction. 'However, since we enjoyed that burst of publicity, things have again taken a downward plunge. A month ago, the Moderator set up a think tank to find out what could be done. I was asked to chair that august body.' He smiled at us and we smiled back. 'After a quite extensive session, the inevitable conclusion reached was that we needed something to excite our members and focus their minds back on to Christianity. Although we all know the thrill of being in the service of our Maker, I'm afraid to say it does not seem to grab a present-day believer as it should do. In short, we need to proselytise them. I think we all agree with that.' Again the others nodded their heads in approval. I nodded mine also and made a mental note to look up proselytise in a dictionary. This necessitated me making another mental note to buy a dictionary.

'Good.' Major Day rose from his chair and, placing his hands in his trouser pockets, slowly walked round to my side of the table and perched on the table just by my side. He removed his hands from his pockets, took a deep breath and, with a new sense of intensity in his voice, continued. 'The end result of this searching was that we, as a Church, had to come up with a strategy. We needed to formulate an event that would raise the profile of our Church to such an elevation that we would be the topic of conversation in every workplace throughout the land. We needed something that would capture the attention of the entire world.' He paused and smiled mischievously. 'But what? Aye, there was the rub. What was that magical something? The talisman that would solve the riddle.' He was staring at the opposite wall as if he was looking straight through it. Suddenly he turned to me and asked, 'Can you guess what we came up with, Jolly?'

I must say he caught me right off guard. 'A raffle?' I suggested. Everyone laughed as if I had made another joke so I laughed again as well.

'That's a right dry sense of humour you have there, Reverend,' Allyson Wonterland said, nodding in approval at me from across the table. 'I like a man that can make me laugh. Takes my mind off my feet, so it does.'

I was dying to ask them what I had said that was so funny but I felt perhaps that I should not so I decided to move the discussion on. 'Did you eventually come up with something that you felt could do the trick?' I said, thereby cleverly steering the discussion back to Major Day

'Let me turn the question back on you, Jolly,' he said, thereby unwittingly sending me into a panic. 'We decided to set ourselves the task of finding the most elusive object in the Christian faith. What we came up with is considered, by most theologians, to be the single most sought after object of Christ's life – the artefact that sent the Knights Templar on a quest that caused a bloody war, costing thousands of lives, yet ended in failure –

the relic that has eluded not only discovery but also even description – setting alight a fever, in the combined brains of men of vision, that none of them have solved. Need I give you any more information on what we are centring on? Do you now have an idea what we feel will bring this about?'

'Well,' I began, tentatively, 'I think I'm going away from my original suggestion of the raffle.' I searched their faces for a clue that I was correct in this suggestion. The only thing I got was the usual puzzled expression. 'So,' I continued, 'would I be a million miles away if I said the word "tombola"?'

After a brief pause, Major Day said, 'I wonder, Jolly, if you would excuse us while we have a private discussion among ourselves. If you would be good enough to wait outside, we will call you back in shortly. Just a few loose ends I would like to put to my colleagues. Would that be all right?' he said with what I thought was an air of overdone offhandedness. 'Just a few nuts and bolts to tighten up before we go any further.'

I have never been much of a handyman so there was no point in offering my assistance. 'Don't be too long, then – it's raining,' I reminded them. As I left the tent, I thought I could hear what sounded like a wee bit of a heated discussion starting. I knew, of course, what was going on. My suggestion of a tombola had probably hit the nail on the head thus making them face up to the fact that their world-shattering scheme was not as surprising as they all thought. I hoped they wouldn't worry unnecessarily, however, as, of course, not everyone would be able to pick up on it as quickly as I had.

The rain hadn't eased up so I decided to pass the time of day with the policeman who was standing outside the tent.

'I see the rain hasn't eased up,' I said conversationally.

'Aye, it hasn't that,' he replied, with a lilt in his voice that suggested he was from the locale.

'You sound like a true man of the mountains. Are you from around here, then?' I continued, guessing that he could do with some company.

'No,' he said, 'I'm just good at accents.'

I decided to test my theory out, regarding the surprise event being argued over inside the tent, on the constable. I was sure that no one would guess it as quickly as me. If I could assure the four of them that a highly trained member of the constabulary was unable to latch on, then it would ease their minds somewhat.

'Tell me, constable, what do you think I am alluding to if I asked you to try and guess the following? I may have to paraphrase a bit but it's roughly right. If your name was TEMPLAR and you were only allowed out at NIGHT to go to some ARTY-FARTY war picture, where thousands of soldiers died and at the end of it you FAILED to know what it was all about, where would you be?'

'Haven't a Scooby,' he replied with an air of total disinterest.

Just as I thought, I thought. 'One last question, constable. Would you think you might be at a tombola?'

'Haven't a Scooby. I hope you're not going to be out here long,' he replied, scowling, obviously concerned that I might catch a chill.

At that the door opened and the Very Reverend Mee popped his head round. 'Would you come beck insed egain, Jolly?' he said, standing aside and ushering me in with his arm.

As I passed him, I said, 'Good news – the constable hasn't a clue what you were on about so it looks as if your secret will remain a surprise.'

'Oh! Thet is re-essuring,' he replied, uncomprehendingly.

The expressions on the faces of Major Day and his two companions were ones of nagging doubt. I could tell this by the give-away signs of Day ringing his hands and biting his lower lip, while Doctor Hwy continually ran his hands distraughtly through his hair. Even Allyson Wonterland had lost her air of distraction. Her lips were pursed and she was rubbing her right foot with the knuckles of her left hand which she had clenched up into a fist. She was also making grunting noises of either agony or pleasure. It was difficult to determine which.

'Please sit down, Jolly,' Major Day said, pointing at the vacant seat on the other side of the table. 'I won't hide anything from you. We were a bit worried that, perhaps – and this is no reflection on you,' he said, looking at me firmly, 'that, perhaps, we had picked the wrong man for the task. It crossed our minds that you may be too stup . . . eh, unworldly, that's the word, not stupid, for the task we had in mind for you.'

My heart sank inside me. Did this mean the end of my dreams of serving my Church and thereby becoming the most famous, not to mention richest, minister in Scotland? Was this the end of my lifelong ambition of maybe even meeting the Moderator? I gazed blankly at the four of them, trying to think of some way of getting myself back in favour. I grasped at the first thing that came to mind, 'Tombola was just a lucky guess, honest.'

'Really?' continued Major Day. 'We had a full, frank and even heated discussion, as you probably guessed.' He stared at me. 'Well, maybe not.' He started to speak slowly, 'When you left, we had another, eh, wee talk as to your suitability. We came to the conclusion that the very naivety, the unawareness that you naturally possess may, in fact, be just the quality that could make the mission a success.' He held out his hand and I did too. As he shook my hand, he smiled, 'We're back on course. Welcome aboard again. There is a private letter that explains all but I'm going to dispense with that. I'm now going to run the whole scheme up the flagpole and let the wind of knowledge fill your sails.' Wisely, I kept quiet.

'We are after no less a prize than the HOLY GRAIL itself – the very cup that Christ drank from at the Last Supper. If we can produce this talisman of the Christian faith and PROVE that it is the genuine article, then we will see a return to

Christianity that will set the Church of Scotland at the forefront of every Church on the planet.'

Much as I considered it wise to keep my thoughts to myself, I felt I had to let them in on one vital point – a basic flaw that they seemed to have overlooked. I put my hand up. 'I'm sorry to tell you but I haven't got it. I don't know who told you I had but, honestly, I haven't. However, if I come across it, I'll let you know,' I said, starting to rise.

'Oh for f . . . fortune's sake, Jolly, we know you don't hev it,' the Reverend Mee cut in, testily. 'Sit beck down.'

'Hellish funny, Reverend,' Allyson Wonterland said with a broad smile. 'You have a great sense of humour. Are you from Glasgow?' I nodded. 'Aye, I thought you might be. If I were you, I would stick the heid on Snow White's wee pal here,' she said, indicating the Very Reverend Mee.

'Why?' I enquired.

'No! No' Hwy – him!' she said, nodding at Mee again.

'Do you mean me?' Mee said, jumping down off his chair.

'Are you Mee?' she glowered at him.

'No! You're you. I'm Mee!' Mee glowered back.

'That's enough,' interjected Major Day. 'There is no need for this. We're at each other's throats and I don't know why.'

'Yes you do,' I butted in, trying to help. 'That's Mister Hwy there. You introduced him to me – remember?'

'It's DOCTOR Hwy,' Hwy broke in.

'I don't care if you're DOCTOR Who, Why, Where or When. Can we get back to WHAT we were talking about?' shouted Major Day.

A silence descended on the small gathering.

'Let's all take a deep breath and remember why . . .' He stopped himself and then, with a warning glower at us, continued, 'Remember the reason we are here.' He rounded on me. 'Jolly, don't say anything else until we have explained fully the exploit we want you to undertake. Is that clear?'

I put my hand up again.

'Yes?' he asked warily.

'Will you nod your head or give me some kind of sign to let me know that you are finished when you are finished?' I asked back equally warily.

'Good idea,' he said. 'I'll point to you like this,' he said pointing at me. 'Will that be all right? Clear enough?' His voice had a tone as if he was talking to a child. 'Just nod if you agree,' he instructed. I nodded.

'Right, then. I'll carry on.' He carried on. 'We kind of took it for granted that the Holy Grail was not in your or anyone else's possession, Jolly, although there are more than a few bodies who lay claim to it. It is our opinion that it still remains undetected despite many attempts to acquire it over the last two millennia. This, indeed, is why we believe that our producing it will be a major coup not only for the Church of Scotland but also for Christianity as a whole. However, we covered most of that earlier. Jolly, you may be aware that . . .' he paused for a moment, staring at me. 'No – you're probably not. I perhaps should fill you in on the various theories that have been going the rounds regarding the Grail.'

He again put his hands in his trouser pockets and turning from the table, started to pace slowly back and forth. 'Most of the received wisdom regarding the Grail is that it was the cup that Christ drank from on the very last occasion he and the apostles were together. As you know, it was at this last gathering that Christ filled his cup with wine and then instructed his followers to drink to his memory – to remind them of their time together and of his ministry and what it stood for. He also said that the wine was, that evening, made blood, his blood, and the bread that they broke was his body. The bread was obviously eaten so no vestige of that remained and likewise the wine.

'This left the cup that Christ drank from as his last possession before he was captured and put to death. It is not unrealistic to

49

think that it would almost certainly have been retained – shall we say? – by someone at that last fateful meal. The early followers of Christ attributed mystical powers to it and, not surprisingly, it vanished. Subsequently, many expeditions, the best known perhaps being those of the crusaders, have tried to find its whereabouts. There have also been many theories as to its actual form. What was it? Was the cup a plain simple wooden or pewter vessel or was it, as some have suggested, a lavish jewel-encrusted cup supplied by some rich convert who had become a follower?

'There is another, in my view, fanciful theory that the inter-pretation of the word Grail means any receptacle which held Christ's blood. The theory is that Mary Magdalene was pregnant with Christ's child and that her belly was the Grail.' A gasp burst from my open mouth. I put my hand up. He shook his head, put his fingers to his lips and continued. 'As I said, fanciful. We, as a body, are in favour of the cup theory. How to produce it? That's the problem. The one thing we can be sure of is that the last definite sighting of it was at that Last Supper. What happened to it? Where is it? If we can answer these questions then we will be, as the Mafioso say, "Made Men".' I noticed he was back to the Latin stuff again but I held myself in check. He turned to face me – 'And that's where you come in, Jolly.'

I could not contain myself. 'I'm not joining the Mafia!' I protested, jumping to my feet.

'Did I point to you?' he asked.

'No,' I replied.

'Then sit down and don't speak. Remember we agreed on that?' he said, scolding me.

My friend Allyson pulled a face, behind his back, which made me laugh. It also made me feel that I was not to be spoken to like a naughty little boy. 'What are you laughing at?' he said, his eyes narrowing.

'It was Allyson, sir. She made me laugh,' I stuttered before I could stop myself.

Major Day whirled round and addressed Allyson, 'Stop making Jolly laugh, Miss Wonterland.'

'Away and fly a canary,' was Allyson's response.

'This whole thing is degenerating into ferce,' said Mee. 'It will never work.'

'Would you like to bet?' said Major Day.

'I am sure he would love Tibet,' said Doctor Hwy, as though he was glad to be able to contribute something at last to the conversation. 'It is a most beautiful country and the people are so friendly . . .'

'QUIET!' Major Day's voice cracked like a whip through the air. 'PLEASE, can we try to concentrate? Do you want to help your Church or don't you? If you do not, then we are all wasting our time. I was under the illusion that we were all here to back the Moderator and his efforts to bring Christ to the forefront of twenty-first-century thought. If, however, I was mistaken in my belief and you are here just to make a mockery of this mission, then I ask you to leave here and now.' His eyes strafed us, waiting for a response. Nobody moved and it's fair to say that we all felt we had let him down.

'Very well, I will continue without, I hope, interruption. I was about to tell you, Jolly, before you broke your promise not to speak, how you could assist in this momentous mission. Do I have your permission to carry on or would you like to continue being a total twerp? The choice is yours.'

I felt the eyes of the others bore into me (except for Allyson's, she had gone back to rubbing her feet). I said I was sorry but crossed my fingers behind my back as I was still determined that the Mafia was not an option.

'Good. Let's get back to the reason we are here,' said Major Day. 'As I was about to tell you, Jolly, this is how you come in. Now please pay attention because this is the most important

51

part of the whole operation. The reason other attempts to locate the Grail have failed is because they could not trace it back to that remarkable night that Christ broke bread for the last time with his companions. We, with your help, Jolly, are going to attempt to do just that. We are going to attempt to place you back in time, back to that momentous night in Jerusalem when the Last Supper was actually taking place. This, Jolly, is why you are here. It's also why you were, and still are, sworn to secrecy. You will live those times in Judea. You will attend the Last Supper and you will witness and then report back to us what happened to the Holy Grail.' He pointed to me. 'Now you can speak.'

I said nothing, owing to the fact that I was speechless. Everyone was looking at me. Even Allyson had stopped rubbing her feet. She gave me a wee smile and said, 'That's nice, eh?'

'Any questions?' Major Day asked – rather unnecessarily, I thought.

'Quite a few,' I replied, equally unnecessarily. 'Why me and how do I do it? Have you got some kind of time machine?'

Major Day looked round the table 'No! There is no time machine. Why you and how do you do it? That's where these good people come in. As you will recall, Doctor Hwy is an expert in metaphysics while Miss Wonterland is a well-respected hypnotist and, to a lesser extent, reader of teacups. It is to them that we will look for the successful outcome to the scenario we have described. Miss Wonterland will attempt to regress you to previous lives that you have inhabited.' He saw my eyebrow shoot up. 'Yes, I know what you are thinking – it sounds like reincarnation and the Church does not recognise such frivolous beliefs.' He passed behind me and patted me on the shoulder. 'Doctor Hwy, perhaps you could take over here and give my friend Jolly the benefit of your knowledge.'

As Doctor Hwy stood up, the material of his black coat crackled. 'My pleasure. Reverend Jolly,' he began, 'in my country, we have, for centuries, believed in reincarnation and it has always been scoffed at. My people tolerated this as it suited them to be left alone anyway. However, science is now beginning to catch up on what we have always known about.' His eyes danced with an ill-disguised pride. 'I will try to make this explanation as simple as possible. Even you may be aware that we are all made from atoms and these atoms are made up of even smaller particles that I will not complicate your reasoning powers with. Suffice it to say that the constituents of these particles are indestructible. They are forever. The same particles of life that were on this planet millions of years ago, are here still. When we die and our remains disintegrate, these tiny fragments re-enter the lifecycle and become a part of existence all over again. Are you following this explanation?'

'Yes,' I lied.

'The easiest way to give you an example of this is to offer the explanation of why we have déjà vu.' He read my mind correctly. 'Déjà vu is when we think we've already been somewhere but can't remember when we went.'

'Is that like if you get up during the night and need to go to the toilet?' I probed.

'In your case, yes! In everybody else's case, no. People sometimes say, "This feels like it has happened to me before." This is because one of these tiny fragments that help to make up the whole person may have once been a memory cell that connects, coincidentally, with another memory cell whizzing around inside his or her brain and then it's gone. But, for that brief moment in time, both those cells will flash a memory of long ago, of times past, to the brain of the present host. This is, in fact, a form of reincarnation.' He paused to let whatever he had been talking about sink in to my brain.

'And it is a form that we believe we can tap into for our own purpose,' continued Major Day. 'Thank you, Doctor Hwy. A precise and erudite explanation if ever I heard one. We are in your debt. As I said, Jolly, we intend to try to send you back through time by hypnotism. Miss Wonterland will try to regress you by hypnotising you – that is by sending you into a deep sleep from which she will coax you to open up and allow us to pry out of your mind some of the oldest memories stored up inside you. As Doctor Hwy has explained, they are all in there. It just depends on how good a subject you turn out to be as to whether we can go that far back.'

I scratched my head. 'Are you still trying to work out what we've been explaining to you,' Major Day enquired.

'No, my head's itchy. I get terrible scoriasis of the scalp when I'm scared stiff,' I informed him. 'What if I get hypnotised and you can't bring me back and how do you know I would have been in Judea at that time anyway?'

'Good question. Well, the world was not such a large place then as it is now,' Major Day started explaining. 'And the Middle East was the place to be if you were a follower of religion. According to Doctor Hwy, we retain the fragments of the atoms that are our driving force throughout our existence. You are a pastor now so it's probable you were some kind of holy man then too. It's true we require a large chunk of luck but we won't know if we're successful until we try. As for being unable to bring you back, I'd better let Miss Wonterland give you assurance on that score.'

'You and I have a lot of simpatico – don't worry, you'll be fine, Reverend.' She looked up from footering about with her feet. 'I'm looking forward to mesmerising you. You're in a trance most of the time anyway so you'll hardly notice the difference.' Still examining her foot, she continued, 'There is one thing I need to know and I need you to answer me truthfully.'

'What's that?' I enquired, with no small amount of trepidation.

She stared deep into my eyes, as though searching for some hint that I might try to hide something from her. She eventually spoke, 'Is that a corn I'm getting? It's right in the middle of my foot so I can't quite see it.' She lifted her leg side-on so I could have a look. A flash of pink bloomers was enough to deter me from any examination. Ephesia had warned me long ago how women could use their subtle feminine wiles to ensnare unsuspecting men. And believe me, when Ephesia warns you, you stay warned.

'No!' I hastily assured her. 'As far as I can make out, it's not a corn.' I knew I was back in the realms of pale untruths but, as I once heard my father remark, 'Better a white lie than a black eye.'

She grabbed my hand. 'Are you sure? You hardly looked. It could just be a bit o' hard skin – have a wee feel and see what you think.' Did the hussy know no shame? Was there no part of her anatomy she would not flaunt in order to seduce an attractive man? Would she take advantage of me while I was in recession (or whatever it was called)? More importantly, would Ephesia find out and give me a seeing-to? These thoughts filled my brain and, along with the other propositions I had become heir to this day, it must have been too much. My head started to spin and, as the room revolved above, I saw Miss Wonterland's hand reach out to me, then all went black.

I seemed to be falling down a dark, sun-forsaken void. As I whirled round and round, I could see figures from history reach and shout out to me as I spun away from them. 'ONE SMALL STEP FOR MANKIND,' shouted Louis Armstrong as he hopped around the moon. Winston Churchill, standing in the halls of Parliament, shouted, 'NEVER IN THE FIELD OF HUMAN CORNFLAKES . . .' and then I wafted away from him. 'I'LL MAKE IT UP TO YOU THE NEXT TIME!' Adolph Hitler bellowed with a smile and a cheery wave as he flashed past.

Then I saw a point of light in the distance. Like an iron filing to a magnet, I was being drawn to it. I tried to shield my eyes from the radiance but it was no use. Irresistibly, it beckoned and I was, indeed, powerless to resist. Never had I seen such radiance. It grew and grew until I thought my eyes would burst. From the light, I could hear a voice speaking to me. The sound of it reverberated in my consciousness, 'Behold-be-hold-hold-hold- . . .'

I came to with the sight of Doctor Hwy shining a light into my eye. 'Hold this torch while I examine his pulse,' Hwy said as he studied me carefully. He had placed a finger on the side of my neck and it felt cool. 'He should be all right in a minute or two.' I heard his voice. It was thin and cold – like Ephesia's soup.

Major Day's face hove into view. 'How are you feeling, Jolly?' His voice sounded distant and far away. He continued talking but not to me. 'I think maybe he had too much information at the one time. Maybe we made a mistake. Perhaps we should think of someone else who can pull off this task. I don't know if he could handle the inevitable fame and riches that will come his way.'

Doctor Hwy continued to focus on my open eye. 'You may be right but I have a feeling that he will prove to be an exceptional subject for the type of regression we have planned.' His finger was still resting on my pulse, his other hand was now feeling the top of my head. I could sense his fingers probing the bumps on my head. 'His skull is remarkable. It's so smooth – as if he had never had a single idea in his entire life.'

I heard Mee's voice jump in, 'How exectly do you mean?'

Hwy replied, 'Let me put it this way – if his brain was a room, it would be unfurnished. He is like the proverbial open book. We will never get a better subject.' The tone of his voice altered. 'He's regaining consciousness – well, as much as he's capable of.'

I certainly was regaining consciousness. The phrase 'We will never get a better subject' had taken root in my head. I now knew what was happening. This was the time I had been born for. 'We will never get a better subject.' I knew my flock needed me. I also knew that I could never turn my back on my Moderator or my Church's hour of need. Lead on Mac-Donald's. Cometh the hour, cometh the minister. Gabriel had blown his own trumpet and I would not flinch in its blast. I WOULD FULFIL MY DESTINY – unless, of course, Ephesia said no.

'Ehr you all rhet, Jolly? We were eh ted worried ehbout you,' said Mee. 'Ken Eh get you eh wee drink of something?'

'Please accept our apologies, Jolly,' Major Day said with a genuine tone of regret in his voice. 'We perhaps got carried away with our enthusiasm for the Holy Grail assignment. It was obviously an enormous shock to your system and, although we would love you to be our man in Judea, we will understand if you would think it *infra dignitatem*. Sorry, Latin again. Annoying, I know. I'm afraid it's the down side of a degree in the classics – I always seem to speak in quotes. It means "below one's dignity".'

'I don't know about the classics,' I explained, 'but I will give YOU a bit of Latin for a wee change. I am maybe not *infra dignitatem* but I am certainly *Infra copperus et infra quidus* and that means "in for a penny, in for a pound".'

The grin on Major Day's face nearly broke it in two. It was the cheeriest I'd made anyone in ages. Seldom have I seen anyone so happy as he went round shaking everyone's hand. We all had a wee cup of tea except for Doctor Hwy who had a cup of *tsampa* which, believe it or not, is Tibetan tea. I have found out since that it is rancid butter floating in hot yak's milk. Don't ask me why Has Mee Hwy preferred it to Typhoo but he did.

For a bit of fun and to relax us all, once we had finished, Allyson read all our teacups. (Except, of course, the Doctor's.) But there wasn't much point really – being good Church of Scotland Protestants none of us believed in that sort of thing.

However, we all drained our cups, gave them a whirl, turned them upside down and then discovered that there was what looked like a tree in the tea leaves. She told Ewen Mee that he was in line for promotion, would never grow tall and had a problem with his bowels. He said the first two were true but that the last one was not. Miss Wonterland said she was never wrong but then corrected herself when she realised that one of the leaves was a V and not a B.

It was Major Day's turn next and he smiled indulgently when she stared into his cup. She shook her head and then told him that he was going to lose all his teeth. 'How do you know that?' he asked, incredulously.

'Because there's a lot of sugar at the bottom of the cup and it's bad for your teeth,' she informed him.

Then it was on to me. She said that Ephesia would leave me and that I was going to be very sorry. I asked her to make up her mind which one was true. I also asked how she could tell my future if she was about to send me back to the past. She pondered on this and then gave me back my teacup. While the others conferred on this point I had my first chance to consider what was in store for me. The foremost thought in my mind, of course, was that I might actually meet the Son of God. What would I say? How would I react? These questions were too much for me to contemplex. I decided, however, to keep my fingers crossed that I would somehow, somewhere, be given the opportunity to meet my Saviour. Then I uncrossed them because Ephesia told me it was bad luck to be superstitious. One thing that did worry me, however, was the thought that, if I was born again, would I have two belly buttons? This set me off on my own little reverie. I had always had an exquisitive mind and had never failed to question the mysteries of existence. If, for example, we are here to help others, why are the others here? How deep would the ocean be if there were no sponges? What should you do if you see an endangered animal eating an endangered plant? When the government gave John Prescott two jags, why wasn't the second one lethal? These were just some of the questions I determined to ask the Messiah should I be fortunate enough to encounter him. I was pulled back from my thoughts by the voice of Major Day calling my name.

'Jolly, would you care to join us over here at the table? We would like to determine a date for your first dice with dea . . . – appointment with destiny. Obviously tomorrow is out.'

'Why?' I enquired.

'It's Sunday. You're eh Church of Scotland Minister, remember?' chipped in Mee as he climbed up on to his chair.

With all that had taken place I had quite forgotten. 'Of course. As a matter of fact, I still have to sort out my sermon. I have no idea what it will be. Everything seems to pale into signifitude now that I am about to embark on the adventure of a lifetime.'

'The adventure of a thousand lifetimes, Reverend Jolly,' Doctor Has Kmee Hwy reminded us.

'Would Monday be alright?' the Major asked, opening one of those organiser things and searching it. 'Do you have a window then?'

'Well,' I informed him, 'where we live may be a bit Sparticus but we do have a window – in fact, we've got two and a door as well.'

'Yes, of course you have! I meant are you free on Monday. Would you have time to try for a first go at it so to speak.'

'Monday!' I yelped. 'Is that not a bit soon? I mean, for God's sake, give me time to catch my breath, will you?'

'Need Eh remehnd you, Jolly, thet it is for God's sake thet we ehr here in the first place or hev you forgotten so soon?' Mee's voice again interjected impatiently. 'Eh mean to say it's not es if you ehr going to the other sed of the continent. You'll just be coming to eh wee flet thet we hev leased in the town. You don't even need to peck eh suitcase.'

'What about sandwiches?'

'You'll no' need sandwiches, Reverend,' purred Miss Wonterland. 'I just want to make a couple of passes at you.'

My worst fears were confirmed. This had to be nipped in the bud. 'May I remind you that I am a married minister, Miss Wonterland. You can make a pass if you like but it will get you nowhere – that is apart from the casualty ward if Ephesia catches you at it.'

She smiled indulgently. 'Awww! How nice! Isn't that lovely?' she said to her three companions. 'Naw! Reverend, when I say pass, all I mean is I'm going to wave my hands in front of your face, to hypnotise you and send you for a nice wee sleep. You'll enjoy it, so you will,' she beamed.

'So, Jolly, shall we say Monday? 10 a.m. to start at 11?' Major Day asked in a way that suggested he had made up his mind already. His pencil was poised over the diary. The Very Reverend Ewen Mee was putting on his coat. Doctor Hwy was buttoning his long black number up. But what really signalled that the meeting was over, done and dusted, was Allyson Wonterland had put on her shoes and had done so with a sharp intake of breath that suggested considerable pain was being tholed. It occurred to me that I would not like to be the one that caused that pain to be lengthened to any degree.

'Aye! Well, I'll just have a look in my diary,' I sniffed, pulling out an old shopping list that Ephesia had given me a week ago. I did my best to disguise its true function by cupping it in my hands and pretending to flip through some pages. I mumbled away to myself, 'Let me see now Monday – Monday. Ah! Here we are. I just hope that – yes, I believe I do have a windpipe open that day.'

'Splendid,' said the Major. 'I am so glad. It's been a very productive day. I feel quite elated – mainly thanks to you, Jolly.'

'Good,' I said. 'I'm glad I made your day, Major Day.'

We moved towards the front flap and soon we were standing

outside in the fresh air. A low rumble in the distance seemed to gather momentum as it mixed with the sound of a lone piper playing a fast tune. The piper was out of sight, hidden from where we were standing by a large marquee, but it was most romantic as the notes swooped and soared in the soft wind.

'I thought the weather seemed to be clearing up but that sounded like thunder,' remarked the Major. I was about to agree when I realised that the thunder was unsuccessfully trying to keep time to the piper. Oh dear! My worst fears started to take a tangible form as I heard the sound of wood creaking and groaning, timbers snapping and collapsing, mixed with the pipes, which were now squealing in agony as though trapped in some vicious snare. The sight of two swords spinning in the air above the marquee confirmed what I had suspected.

'I think that may be the Highland dance contest finishing,' I said by way of an explanation. 'I'll just collect my wife and lend a hand with the first aid. See you all on Monday then. Cheery bye.'

As I picked my way through the broken limbs and human debris that inevitably followed Ephesia's attempts to dance, I could not help but admire the grit and determination she showed as she still manfully hopped and pranced among the human flotsam that was all that remained of the judges.

Ephesia had decided to appeal, quite rightly I felt, against the judges' decision to ban her from all future events at the Braemar Games. I fully supported her in her appeal. First because I had never found her appealing before and I thought I should take the opportunity to do this at least once in our relationship. And secondly because I felt she was being victimised by her fellow combatants. The argument was that, as Ephesia was winning so easily, the other combatants were made to feel incombatant and she was, therefore, infringing on their human rights. Also, when the marquee collapsed during her attempt at the sword dance, thirty-eight illegal economic refugees and four ex-Taliban fighters were trapped and they were suing the Games' authority for not supplying adequate shelter while they were hiding from this repressive government.

While the lawyers were phoning their banks to make adequate provision for their ever-swelling coffers and issuing statements to the press on how they would fight to the death to protect democracy and the right of any lawyer, no matter where they came from, to make a killing at the tax-payer's expense, I took a wee walk around the various stalls and exhibits to pass the time. There seemed to be hundreds of marquees all offering various attractions. Unfortunately, most of them were tractors and, therefore, no use to me.

I stopped at one, just to be polite. A long trestle-type table, covered with at least four soaking-wet white tablecloths tacked on to it, to stop them blowing away in the wind, protected the marquee's entrance. Various pots of jam were spread out on the cloths, along with photographs of past Games and the people who attended them, books on the region, etc.

However, one object caught my eye and almost made it and its companion jump out of their sockets. It was situated at the rear of the table and was under the protection of a large lady who was under the protection of a brown waxed waterproof coat and a brown waxed waterproof hat. The hat was perched on top of a hairstyle resembling a very large Brillo pad. Her face comprised of various hues due to the fact that the rain had caused her black eyebrow pencil to run on to her purple eye shadow, which then was unsuccessfully trying to blend with the puce-toned blusher on her cheeks. This had followed the basic rules of plumbing by following gravity and running down her cheeks, there to merge with her vermilion tinted lips. The whole effect was set off by a face powder that seemed to be made up from two of sand and one of cement.

What had drawn my attention was a silver cup. It was just an ordinary silver cup and normally I would not have given it a second glance. However, my gaze was irresistibly drawn to it because on the front of it were the initials 'H G'.

I could hardly contain my excitement. Was this it? Did the initials stand for Holy Grail? Had I stumbled, by accident, on the most sought after relic in Christendom here at the Braemar Games? I had to play the next part of this scenario exactly right or I might blow my chances of immortality and a few bob in the bank right out of the water.

'Good afternoon, Miss Lopez. I wonder – if it's not too cheeky – might I have your autograph?' I wheedled.

'I'm sorry, Reverend, but I think you have maybe went and mistook me for someone else,' replied the object of my flattery, showing no sense of grammatical construction.

I pressed on, 'Of course, I understand you want to remain hyroneymous. But tell me, J.Lo, that silver cup there, do the initials stand for Holy Grail?'

'No,' she replied with a blush and, in doing so, added to the multicoloured kaleidoscope that was now her face. 'They stand for Hugh Grant. He's went and become the chieftain for the day, so he has, and this is a wee pressy from us by the way of us thanking him for being the day's chieftain. You didn't really think I was Jennifer Lopez, did you?' she asked, smiling at me.

'No! I just wanted to find out what H G stood for,' I said glumly.

She was still calling me for everything nasty she could think of when I heard Ephesia call out my name – thus signalling she was ready to leave. 'I'm sorry but I must go now. Can I count on seeing you at church tomorrow?' I think she may have guessed how crestfallen I was because I heard her refer to me as a miserable pastor to a companion who had come out to find out what all the noise was.

As I left the games with Ephesia, I could see the ruins of the Highland dance section. Apparently the reason for the scene of mayhem was that, when one tent collapsed, there was a slight domino effect. Fortunately, the first aid tent, where the majority of the contestants were lining up outside to be attended to, had not been damaged. Most of their ills were simply strains brought about by trying to match Ephesia for sheer strength. The scene brought to mind the book of Exodus XL:2:

> And the Lord spake unto Moses, saying, 'On the first day of the first month shalt thou set up the tabernacle of the tent of the congregation.'

Unfortunately, the toilet facilities did not survive, which brought to mind Deuteronomy XXXIII:

> He that shall have his privy member cut off, shall not enter into the congregation of the Lord.

So that did not bode well for a large turn out at church tomorrow.

Sunday was like Saturday – a complete washout and a very poor attendance at services. Now Monday had arrived and I was in no fit state for the task ahead. I could not sleep last night for thinking about what terrors lay in front of me. Actually what was lying beside me was pretty terrifying too. Ephesia didn't so much snore as roar. I usually try to ignore her snore but last night the roar of her snore shook the door. I wish she could snore in semaphore or, better still, in Singapore, furthermore and forevermore.

I lay awake remembering when we were young and she first told me I was in love with her. I thought then that court-ship was like the beautiful pictures in a seed catalogue. Unfortunately, marriage is like what actually comes up. Of course, when all is said and done, at the end of the day, relationships are all a matter of chemistry, which is probably why Ephesia treats me like toxic waste.

I read in a science book that most men die before their wives. The book's explanation was that the stress of providing for a family and bad dietary habits were possible causes. I just think they want to.

Adam and Eve probably had the perfect marriage, because he didn't have to listen to her talk about all the other men she could have married and she wasn't ever compared to his mother.

It made a change for me to be the one who couldn't nod off as Ephesia is the one who has always suffered from troubled and disruptive sleep patterns. She tends to shift about seeking a nice wee bit in our bed. This might be due to her continuous complaint that she very seldom got a wee bit in the bed. She said going to bed with me reminds her of holidays – they never seem to last long enough and are always finished too soon. Which just goes to show that the romance has not left our marriage.

But last night she was amazingly still and at rest. This was not so much that she had found some inner peace but more likely because she mistook a packet of plaster of Paris for bath powder. I have always had a strange and unreasonable fear of women, which is probably why I took up with Ephesia.

These thoughts and more troubled my slumber until, eventually, I got up and made myself a cup of Ephesia's worm-flavoured coffee. The advantage of Ephesia's coffee was that it did not keep you awake as there was no caffeine in it. The reason for this was that there was no coffee in it either. And now Monday was here and my appointment with destiny had arrived. As I made my way to the designated flat, which the Very Reverend Ewen Mee had given me the address of, my feelings were a mixture of panic mixed up with a heady excitement.

Eventually, I arrived early – just before 10 a.m. The address I arrived at was a substantial building with a plaque outside informing the onlooker it was late Georgian and the late Lord Saivus had stayed there. It seemed I was the only thing that was on time. A card was Sellotaped to the door stating that a Church of Scotland yoga class was being held inside – obviously a cover for what was really going on. I must admit I felt a bit like Sean Canary. The front door was large and solid framed. The wood was of a dark oak consistency and so highly polished that I could make out my outline in the gloss that emanated from it. There was a solid brass knocker in the form of a lion's head that looked down on a horizontal brass letterbox. To the right of this on the wall, an old-fashioned bell pull sat proud of the doorframe. Underneath the bell, it said 'PULL' so I did.

Even from outside, I could hear the harsh clang of clapper on brass clatter about inside a hallway. The door was eventually opened and what looked like a redundant school jannie peered out from behind a pair of unbelievably bushy eyebrows that moved up and down independently of each other. The brows almost wholly obstructed the view of two tiny eyes that squinted from behind a pair of bottle-thick black-framed spectacles. A nose, that looked as if it had been thrown at him through a can of red paint and had just kind of stuck there, supported the spectacles. The legs of the spectacles vanished behind two ears, one of which appeared to be upside down. What passed for a mouth was almost totally hidden by a tobacco-stained walrus moustache that was matched by his tobacco-stained middle-parted hair. When he opened his mouth to speak, I could see that his teeth were the least attractive part of him.

A cigarette of the roll-up variety was balanced precariously on his bottom lip. It quivered when he spoke. The words seemed to swish around soaking up saliva before finally escaping from behind the three brown tombstones that were masquerading as teeth – one at the top and two at the bottom.

'You here for the yoghurt classes?' he shouted. 'Somebody

has went up the stairs already.' His eyes traversed my person. 'You might have left it a bit late.'

'I'm actually early,' I informed him from a distance. 'I'm not due till ten.'

'I didnae mean the day,' he squished through his soggy and fast dismantling fag end, 'I meant in life. Yoghurt cannae perform miracles, you know. I'm Shug. I'm the custodian for this dump.' He pointed up a flight of stairs. 'Up there, first door on your left. You workin' or are you oan the dole?' he enquired, his head going down as his eyebrows went up.

'I certainly am working. I am, in fact, a Church of Scotland minister,' I told him – maybe a bit haughtily – as I climbed the stairs.

'Ach, well,' he said, sympathetically. 'Jobs are hard to come by the noo – mebbe the yoghurt will help. If you need anything, let me know although I'll probably be too busy to help. OK? Right. That's me away into the office to cough my lungs up.' With that he turned around and, as he creaked towards his lair, he started the prelims to coughing his lungs up. When I got to the top of the stairs, I knocked firmly on the door designated by Shug.

'Come in,' the unmistakable voice of Major Day beckoned. As I opened the door, I could see him standing at a large tea urn. 'Just waiting for it to boil,' he informed me. 'And then we can have a cuppa before we begin what may turn out to be the most important day in our history. Take a seat. This shouldn't be too long,' he beamed, nodding towards the urn. 'The others should be along shortly.'

'Thanks very much,' I said, removing my coat and hanging it next to his on a coat rack behind the door. 'I met the caretaker. He told me where you were.'

'Oh, good,' he replied abstractly, lifting the lid from the top of the urn. A cloud of steam rose from it and this seemed to please him no end. 'Right! That's us on the way,' he said with the air of a man who had just finished an extremely important task. He grabbed a large white mug with four thick blue bands ringing it. 'What's your poison – tea or coffee?'

'Tea, please,' I replied.

'Anything in it?' he asked, pouring the water into the mug.

'Tea, please,' I said, before remembering that it was not my dear wife who was being mother and, therefore, it would be proper tea and not one of Ephesia's blends.

He smiled at my reply, obviously mistaking it for an attempt at humour. 'I'm glad to see you're so relaxed about the day, Jolly.'

'I don't mind admitting I hardly slept last night. As I lay in bed, the significance of today's experiment coursed through my every thought. I was in a state of high stimulation the entire night.'

His eyes adopted a faraway look and, as if in reverence, he murmured, 'Being married, it's a long time since I had a night like that.'

A knock at the door signified the timely arrival of another of our intrepid band. The door swung open without benefit of invitation from the Major and Allyson Wonterland teetered in. 'Oh! Thank God for a seat! My feet are murderin' me.' She headed for a chair and sat on it without even removing her coat. 'Ah! That's better,' she sighed, removing her shoes. 'Oh! The relief. I cannae tell you,' she told us. 'Is that tea?' she enquired, quite needlessly, I thought, as it was rather obvious.

'Yes. Would you like a cup?' smiled the Major.

'Oh! I could murder a cup,' she said, threateningly (if you were a cup, that is). 'Milk and three sugars if it's no' too much trouble.'

Major Day started pouring out another mug. This one was yellow with white rings. 'No trouble at all, Miss Wonterland – a Salvation Army member is never happier than when we are pouring out cups of tea.'

'What about when you're saving souls?' I interjected.

'Oh! Yes, of course, saving souls and pouring cups of tea. Though not necessarily in that order.' He glanced at his watch. 'I hope the others haven't been held up.' He walked over to Miss Wonterland and handed her the mug.

'Don't worry, Major,' Miss Wonterland said, soothingly. 'I had a wee read at my tea leaves this morning and there was nothing foreboding in them. The truth is in the tea – as my mother used to say – and, this morning,' she paused for effect, 'I used PG Tips which I have found to be particularly reliable,' she explained, reassuringly, to me.

'I never realised that,' I said.

'Oh! Aye, Reverend Jolly. The leaves don't lie. What brand o' tea does your wife use?'

'I'm not sure. I think it's best described as herbal,' I said, guardedly.

'Ah! That'll no' be so accurate then,' she replied, with a sad little shake of her head. 'I'll have a wee look at your cup before we begin the regression. Just to reassure you.' I, of course, as a man of God, did not believe in any of this mumbo-jumbo.

'What kind of tea are you using, Major,' I asked.

'Eh! Scottish Blend,' he said, glancing at the large catering pack of tea nestling at the side of the urn. I glanced anxiously at Miss Wonterland. She picked up my signal and gave me a thumbs-up sign.

At this point, the door opened without anyone knocking and Has Kmee Hwy and Ewen Mee entered together.

'Good, everyone is here,' sighed the Major. 'Tea, Reverend Mee and Doctor Hwy?'

'Eh! Tea for me,' said Mee.

'Not for me,' said Hwy. 'I had a bowl of steaming hot *tsampa* and some cabbage-coated yak's fat before I left.' We all smiled at him as our stomachs turned in unison.

'Ehr you looking forwerd to your wee edventure then, Jolly?'

69

smirked Ewen Mee as he climbed up on to a perfectly normal-sized chair.

'Oh, yes, I am. Watch you don't fall,' I replied, caringly, but, at the same time, sardonically. His eyes narrowed as he tried to decide whether to give me credit for being sardonic or whether he thought that it was beyond me.

'Were you being serdonic there, Jolly?' He asked, challengingly.

'What's sardonic?' I asked, sardonically, thus confusing both him and me.

'Never mhend,' he said, trying to look in charge of the situation.

Has Kmee Hwy put his hand over his mouth and burped – understandably, considering what he had just had for breakfast.

I decided to change the flow of the meeting. 'I just hope that I am a good subject like you say, Allyson. I always thought that people who were easily put under the influence of a hypnotist were a bit weak-willed and feckless.'

They all looked at each other as if I had said something stupid. 'Is that not the case, then?' I continued, fixing my gaze on Allyson. I don't quite know what happened next but it was as if I lost track of myself for a moment. Because, when she answered me, I was standing on one leg in the corner of the room, clucking like a chicken.

'Not at all, Reverend Jolly,' she assured me, snapping her fingers for some reason. This had the effect of bringing me back to my seat and it also stopped me doing the clucking thing. I noticed that my four companions were smiling and nodding at each other so I presumed they were all reassured that I was neither weak-willed nor feckless.

'You're certainly not weak-willed nor feckless,' said Major Day, encouragingly.

'You have feck to spare, Reverend Jolly,' Has Kmee Hwy concurred.

'Are you sure?' I queried. I had an uneasy feeling that I had missed something.

'Oh, yes,' joined in the Very Reverend Mee. 'In fect, the caretaker told us he hed just told the world's number one fecker where to go.'

'Yes, he did show me the way up here, right enough. That was very nice of him to say that about me, wasn't it?' Everyone agreed by vigorously nodding their heads and snorting with what seemed like suppressed laughter. I suppose they were told not to make too much noise so they had to suppress their relief that I was definitely the right man for the job in hand.

'Well, now that that's sorted and out of the way, let's get down to why we are here. Miss Wonterland can you explain to us what your modus operandi will be?' Major Day glanced at me and seemed to make his mind up about something or other before continuing. 'That is to say, how will you go about the regression and what effect will it have on Jolly when he is in contact with his past?'

'That's a good question,' Allyson said, staring at her shoeless feet and trying vainly to wiggle her toes. 'I'm gonnae put Reverend Jolly in a very deep trance. This will, I hope, have the effect of sending him far back into his past. Now, how far back he goes is anybody's guess. At this stage, it's basically suck it and see. However, once we've sucked it and seen it, we'll have a better idea o' what to expect. As you've all witnessed, he is an ideal subject so I think we might be in for somethin' a wee bit special.'

Major Day thanked her and then turned to Doctor Hwy. 'Anything you would like to add before we begin, Doctor?'

'In Tibetan metaphysics, we discount nothing. All is possible. It will depend on whatever atomic memory particle Jolly focuses on. This will determine where his memory bank will lead him. We do require him to go very far back in time. So, maybe, when Miss Wonterland is giving him guidance when she puts him under, that could be her last suggestion. I would also ask her to suggest that Jolly be given instruction to remember everything that happens to him so he can relate it back to us. Otherwise our exertions might go unrecorded and the information we require could be lost forever.' Everyone agreed that was highly desirable.

Major Day arose from the chair as he again glanced at his watch. 'We are slightly ahead of our schedule to begin at eleven o'clock. But, frankly, I don't see any advantage to putting off what we all want to try to accomplish. So I'm going to ask for a show of hands that we begin without delay. All in favour raise their right hand.' He surveyed us and then said, 'Good. Why have you got both hands up, Jolly?'

'One to say that I agree to starting early and the other to ask if I can go to the toilet. I'm a bit worried that there may be a lack of proper facilities should I succeed in going very far back into the past,' I explained.

'Good thinking, Jolly. I daresay that a toilet break might, in fact, suit everyone. It's that kind of attention to detail that will make or break this venture.' The Major flashed me a congratulatory nod and then dismissed us all for fifteen minutes.

Once we were all back, Allyson Wonterland sat me down in the most comfortable chair in the room, next to which was a table. Major Day placed an old-fashioned spool-type tape recorder on top of the table.

'Just relax, Reverend.' She sat down in front of me. 'Don't worry about a thing. Just to reassure you, I've started to read your tea leaves and they tell me that you are going on a long journey. Now this journey you are going on will be very enlightening for you and everyone connected with you.' She showed me the usual tree that the leaves had formed. 'Can you see that? That tells me you have nothing to worry about at all. So that's nice, isn't it?'

Her voice sounded so calming that I admit I did start to lose my inhibitions and I began to feel that I was quite looking forward to whatever came about. I looked up at Allyson. 'Do you mind if I call you Allyson?' I said. Her eyes looked so warm and friendly that I felt I was sinking into them.

'Not at all, Reverend. I bet you're starting to feel a wee bit sleepy, eh?'

I tried, unsuccessfully, to stifle a yawn, 'I'm afraid I am, Allyson and on and on and on. That was a tele-advert. I remember it from when we used to have the telly. Of course, that was when we had electricity as well. That was before we were relocated up to Pariah's Peak.' I stifled another yawn. My eyelids felt very heavy.

I heard Allyson's voice again. It was very far away but I could hear it. 'Och, you're just about away, aren't you?' she said from somewhere inside my head. 'Just before you drift off, I want to remind you that you must try and get as far back as possible to your first recollections. Try to find the first ever memory you have and store it so that you will remember it for ever and ever.' Her voice sounded so reassuring. 'If you feel you are in any danger, just shout my name. Just shout "Allyson!" and I will snap my fingers and all the danger will vanish. So what do you shout out if you feel you are in danger?'

'Allyson?'

'That's right. Now, you just let everything go and enjoy going down into the deepest part of your memory. Down, down – deep, deeper and deeper. As you go deeper down, my voice starts to fade and the deeper you go you can hardly hear my voice.' I could just about make out what she was saying. 'But I'll always be here for safety. Don't let any . . . '

❖   ❖   ❖

I feel wonderful. I haven't felt like this before – ever. I seem to be floating in a big enormous something? I can't describe it but it is awful nice. I feel as if I'm moving – no that's not quite accurate. I feel as if this big enormous wonderful something is moving. I don't have to do anything. All I have to do is enjoy being here. I can see hundreds, no, millions of wee sparks. They are flying about what looks like hundreds of millions of stars. Each time a spark hits a star, the star lights up spectacularly. That seems to be happening almost everywhere. What a display! Maybe it's New Year's Eve here – wherever here is. It seems to me that one of these star things is getting hit by more sparks than the others. It really is getting brighter than all the others. So bright that it is attracting my attention to the exclusion of everything else. It really is absorbing sparks by the thousands. And the light emanating from within it is so beautiful that it is impossible to resist it. That's probably what is making all the sparks go there. I seem to be among the sparks now, almost as if I was one of them. I feel absolutely brilliant and I really do mean brilliant. HERE WE GO, HERE WE GO, HERE WE GO.

WHERE AM I? I've stopped, I know that, and the brightness is still here but I can't get any bearings. I have no points of recognition.

I seem to be in a large white room. The room is soothingly bright but, as I look round, I can't see any lights. I realise slowly that I am flat out. I also realise that I am not on the floor or on a bed. I am suspended. I am suspended in mid-air. My arms reach out and explore the surroundings. There is absolutely nothing tangible holding me up. Strangely I have no fear.

Somehow or other I feel at home in these surroundings. A form appears in the brightness and I know that I am no longer alone. I can sense a touch so gentle on my brow that it is more like a breeze than a hand. A voice to match that sublime softness pervades my senses. 'Time for you to meet the Council. I hope you feel suitably rested and charged, Ad-Im Jo-Lee.' My eyes rest on a large well-proportioned figure. I know this man – though how I know him I don't know. It is as if part of me knows where and what I am while another part of me is observing the part that knows what is happening. This is strangely NOT confusing for me.

'Thank you. Have you any idea what it is the Council wish to see me about?'

'No,' he replies, in the same soft tone that I notice that I now speak with as well. 'I was instructed to prepare you in readiness for their briefing, Ad-Im Jo-Lee. I'm afraid that is all I know.'

'You have done a good job on preparing me. Thank you, Snoo-Kum-Z.' He nods his agreement. I observe the new me observing the image of himself/myself on some kind of panel that seems to have appeared from nowhere in particular. The image is fixed so, as I walk round it, I can see myself from all angles. I look well and nod to my image in recognition, 'You look good.'

What throws me slightly is my image nodding back and saying, 'Tazalot,' before disappearing.

'I will visit with the Council now, Snoo-Kum-Z.'

Raising his arm, he says, 'I hope all goes well for you. And I will see you the next time you come in for servicing.' He seems to slowly melt away and I am alone. I too begin to melt away and find myself inside a long white tunnel. I walk purposely for a short while and then suddenly turn left and melt through the wall of the tunnel. I am in some kind of chamber. Another soft voice fills the void, 'The Council is ready for you, Ad-Im Jo-Lee. Procedure is starting.'

Four large heads appear in the chamber. They all speak at the same time but with different emphases which has the effect of sounding like they are speaking in harmony – a bit different from Labour Party Councillors is my first thought. The words that they greet me with are not entirely unfamiliar. 'The Council have a task for you, Jo-Lee, which, if you decide to accept it, will mean that the Council will not press you for the unpaid tax that is showing up on your account.' It is the first time I have ever had a final demand in four-part harmony.

'How much do I owe and is the task a difficult one?' I hear the new me enquire.

'You owe a stack. However, the task is a very pleasing one,' reply the Quadronairs.

'Surely I don't owe a stack – there must be some mistake,' I find the new me pleading – in a manner very like the old me.

'We have your account in our heads and there is no mistake. You missed your first payment of ten wee dods of dosh – ten wee dods added together make one fair wee bit. You still didn't pay anything for that year and that made ten fair wee bits that you were in arrears. Ten fair wee bits add up to make one big dod of dosh. You were asked to pay the big dod six months ago with added interest at a levy of one whack of dosh a month. This has not been paid. Added together, the sums outstanding amount to, as we said, a stack of dosh. Consequently, you owe the Council the sum of one stack of dosh. To save you the trouble of making an appeal, we have decided there is no need for one as your Council is in perfect harmony with their decision,' they say, finishing at the same time and with perfect pitch.

I shake my head and address the Council, 'There is no way that I can raise a stack . . .'

The Council interrupts me, 'You have not thanked us for saving you the trouble of making an appeal against our un-animous decision, Jo-Lee. That carries an automatic fine of a WAD OF DOSH.'

It occurs to me that I am not going to be successful in any kind of plea-bargaining stratagem and should throw myself at the mercy of the Council. It also occurs to me never to complain about my Council Tax again. Tommy Sheridan would have had a bring-BACK-the-Poll-Tax campaign with this lot.

I go into familiar wheedling mode territory. 'I am in a state of shock at forgetting to thank the wise and merciful Council for saving me from appealing against a decision that is far reaching in its consequences for world justice. The equity of it all leaves me speechless.'

'And, unfortunately, doshless as well,' croons the Council. 'Which takes us to the task. Actually, it takes you to task or, more accurately, to take on a task to relieve you of the consequences of being doshless which, as you may or may not be aware, are not even to be thought of. The task we have for you involves banishment from our beautiful planet Alpha Sispens in the exquisite constellation of Lushus Gorgeus and being exiled to a total dump of a planet we have decided to call Earth which is in the crappy constellation of Cornus Capicus.'

I hear myself cry out in protest, 'I thought you said it was going to be very pleasing.'

'It is for us – because we're getting rid of you,' chorus the Council. 'We have decided to try to lay the grounds for a possible migration to this Earth in case our own Alpha Sispens ever runs out of resources. We applied for permission to the Master of All Things in Everywhere and the Master bombarded it with space dust quite a while ago – thus bringing life and some form of natural evolution to the place. However, they seem to be stuck and can't get past a form of life whose only interest is swinging about from some kind of tall structures that seem to abound in the place. That and picking at each other's skin and swallowing whatever it is they've picked. Absolutely disgusting.'

This is turning into something more than just a bad hair day. 'What on Alpha Sispens am I supposed to do on this planet. Can't the Master just sort it out? How am I supposed to help with their evolution? There's nothing I can provide that they won't have already.'

I'd never heard sniggering in harmony until that moment. 'Well, that's where you are wrong,' the Council snigger. 'Remember the bit where we said they were stuck? The Master wants someone to get past where they are now and mingle with these creatures, that are content to swing and swallow, and make them more like us. Except, of course, they'll be a lot less attractive. To that end you will be the – em, what's the best way to put this? – catalyst? The Master wants you to find a suitable candidate on the dump, sorry, Earth and – eh – you know . . .' The Council continued with their synchronised sniggering.

'Surely I can take someone from Alpha Sispens to mate with?'

''Fraid not,' is the chorus. 'The evolution side of things would not quite pan out right,' howl the happy harmonisers.

I fall to my knees. 'Can I come back once I've done what the Master wants?'

'Providing it all goes smoothly. Don't see why not. It's up to you really. Get the job done,' snigger, 'and that will be your unpaid tax demand sorted. But you will have to stay there until the Master is satisfied. Look on the bright side – at least you won't have to look your best,' the Council concords with a group giggle.

Getting up from my knees, I have to find out one more thing before I bow to the inevitable. 'What happens to me if I don't accept the task and I also don't pay the tax arrears?'

A simultaneous sharp intake of breath swooshes round the chamber. 'Well, in that event, you will give us no option but to send you to another planet that we were thinking of colonising. We say "were" because it proved vastly more unappealing than even Earth did. It was so unappealing and awesomely awful that nobody has ever elected to go there. In fact, evolution halted at the crawling in the dust stage.' They pause for effect. 'You know, snakes, worms and the place is literally crawling with lice. In fact, it's so lousy with lice that we didn't even give it a full name – we just call it L for lousy.' They had a group grooh.

I ask if, maybe, it would be a shorter stay there because it was much worse than Dust or Earth or whatever it was called. They shake their heads in perfect time and tell me I would be there forever – that I could not go to L and back.

However, there is some scant consolation in the fact that I am told that, if I throw myself at the mercy of the Council, they will fix it so that I will only have a very dim memory of Alpha Sispens. This apparently has the added bonus of making me a very dim memory for them.

They will arrange for all but a tiny fraction of my DNA to be erased. That, they surmise, will make the new place a bit more bearable. There is, of course, only one avenue open to me. 'When and how do I leave?' As soon as possible is the instruction of the Council. I am informed that the transporter is being made ready and, as soon as my DNA is altered, I will be prepared for transportation to the new land.

The Council's countenances fade from sight and I am left to ponder my new set of circumstances. I feel a bit uneasy – as though I am being watched. I watch myself feeling uneasy as if I was being watched. I realise that I am the one making myself uneasy because I am watching myself and decide to stop watching and leave myself to myself. This has the effect of making me feel that I am no longer being watched.

Now I feel lonely. This feeling is not allowed to grow because, suddenly, I am no longer in the Council chamber. I am drifting through various substances and colours until I come to rest in a place that is imbued with a feeling of well-being. The light source is a stunning mixture of violet and purple hues. A deep all-embracing mix of soft vermilion-backed blues that just make me want to float around aimlessly in total and utter abandonment of any worries that I think I may recently have had.

I am still in this state of quiet joy when I feel a light touch on the side of my head. 'Time to leave, Ad-Im Jo-Lee. The Council has instructed us that your memory has to be closed down. You can see the instruction here above you.' I see a line of letters suspended in the air that make up the words 'MEMORY-CLOSE-IT'.

'You are now in the place we call the CLOSE-IT. Soon it will be time for you to come out of the CLOSE-IT and set out on your journey to the dump they've called Earth. My name is Gord-On-Evan. I may be the last thing you will ever hear. If it is, then I wish you well in whatever your future may bring.' The voice seems to be made of silk that rests on my ears like gossamer threads.

'Tazalot,' I reply. 'Gord-On-Evan . . . I'll never forget you.'

I read another line of letters suspended in the air that made up the words 'STAND-BY-TO-TRANSPORT-THIS-LOSER'. Then I feel as though I am some kind of liquid in a vessel that is being whisked from the inside. It is as if a giant finger has been placed inside me and is stirring me round and round until I am swirling so much I can't tell whether I am upside down, inside out or backside foremost.

It is unbelievably scary and then I have a vision of some small furry creature with big eyes and round ears and the body is entirely covered with hair. A name dances tantalisingly round what is left of my consciousness – Ted-something. I can't quite focus on it but, strangely, I feel that this weird creature can somehow help in this maelstrom of emotions that I find myself in. There is another name I am desperately trying to home in on. Somewhere, amongst all the swirling atoms and cell structures, I know that, if I shout out this name, all will be well and I won't have to suffer this agony any longer. What is it? Is it Gord-On-Evan? No! It isn't that. If I can just remember, then all this onslaught will be gone. Wait, I seem to recognise a phrase. What did I say? Something about all this onslaught. All this onslaught? All this onsl-. All this on-. All is on-. Of course, that sounds right – it is Allys-.

Where am I? What am I? Why am I lying stark naked on the ground in the dust. How did I get here?

TRANSCRIPT FROM THE JOLLY TAPES

What this next bit is is a record of what was going on while Miss Wonterland had put me in recession. Fortunately, the tape recorder lived up to its name and recorded their conversation. So I have an actual account of what they were saying. It is actually quite boring just listening to the words, so I have sexed it up a bit by describing, from my own imagination, if their faces screwed up, if they were standing or sitting, etc. In all modesty, I think it makes it a lot better than just writing down bare what was said. I don't like writing bare anyway – it can get very cold up here in the winter. So, if it's all right with you, I'll just do that with all the bits that have been recorded during my recessions.

This was their reaction from when I left Alpha Sispens and found myself on Earth at not quite the beginning of time but really very, very near to it.

'I think he's passed out again,' the voice belonged to Major Day.

'It's not surprehsing,' chimed in Ewen Mee. 'What in heaven's name is going on. Eh ken't make head nor tail of it.'

Doctor Has Kmee Hwy spoke with a voice that seemed to rasp with tension inside his throat. 'In heaven's name? A very interesting phrase, considering what we have just been listening to.'

'Excuse me, I'm just gonnae rub my feet. They're loupin', so they are,' was Miss Wonterland's response.

'What do you mean an "interesting phrase"?' Major Day's question was obviously aimed at Doctor Hwy.

'You must see what's happening here!' Hwy rasped, 'and, if it is true, then the implications are colossal.'

There was no reply.

'Very well, I'll spell it out to you. We asked Jolly to go as far back as possible in his memory. We forgot that his mind is –' he hesitated before carrying on, 'to put the most favourable slant I can on it – his mind is amazingly free of joined-up thought.' (There was an uncalled-for, I thought, murmur of agreement from the rest of the geniuses.) 'This vacuum, that pervades Jolly's brain, has allowed him to go back in time further than anyone in the history of regression – back to a time when there were no traces of human beings on this planet. He talks of the Master of All Things in Everywhere that created life on Earth. In other words he is describing a Supreme Being. This Being caused dust from space to settle on the Earth thus making life possible on the planet. Science knows now, of course, that the essential elements, that make life possible, came from the dust of meteorites smashing into our planet from far off in the solar system. To this day, the Earth is bombarded by dust from space.'

There was another heavy silence in the room, broken finally by Ewen Mee, 'Eh'm efraid Eh'm beginning to see where we're heading with this.'

'Carry on, Doctor Hwy,' the Major said fearfully.

'We have heard Jolly describe his earliest recollections. Follow his story and compare it with what the received wisdom about our world is. We know that, for millions of years, life evolved from a very low form to its present state. We can tell from fossil records that the dominant forms on Earth were the dinosaurs. They ruled this planet for many millions of years. Then something happened to wipe them and all but the most basic life forms out. Some say a gigantic meteorite struck the planet thus bringing about an ice-age that

did not allow them to survive. Others argue that some
virulent disease took a terrible toll on them – the
theories are many.

'What is not in dispute is that it happened and, after
it happened, life started again. It started because the
lowest creatures were not wiped out by the catastrophe
that befell the high and mighty. The worms and
centipedes and crawling insects were numerous so, with
no recognised predators, they gained dominance.
Gradually, mammals evolved and continued to change
and diversify and this led to the apes. From the apes,
there is an unexplained gap till we humans appeared.
Of course, no one to this day can pinpoint that moment.
Or maybe I should rephrase that statement by adding
"UP" to this day. The Old Testament is widely
disbelieved by even the established Churches. Many
leading clergymen have publicly said that it is merely a
collection of fables, not to be taken literally. If what Jolly
is telling us in his regressive state is true, he may be
describing Genesis and they may have to revise their
judgement.'

'Carry on, Doctor,' the Major urged, not realising he
was quoting from one of my favourite films.

'Very well,' replied Hwy. 'The jump from apes to
humans is usually explained away by a theory called
the missing link.'

'I've heard o' that,' Miss Wonterland interjected.
'But I always thought it was to do wi' a robbery in a
sausage factory.'

Wisely, no one said a thing. Hwy's voice continued,
'This missing link is thought to be some kind of
accidental hybrid that took place in the ape culture.
However, if Jolly's descriptions of events are true and
not the ravings of a dysfunctional lunatic, then we may

be witnessing the solution to a mystery that has baffled the combined minds of humankind since civilisation began. He has told us his name is Ad-Im Jo-Lee,' he paused a while. 'I'm sure I am not the only one who has made the connection of his first two names with the Bible's Adam.'

'Oh. Right enough, so it is – and Im Jo-Lee is the same as I. M. Jolly,' Miss Wonterland discovered.

Ewen Mee's voice was tremulous when he said, 'Ehr you suggesting thet Jolly is the original Edem? Because, if you ehr, then the implications of thet ehr too horrible to conjure with. Do you realez thet thet would mean the entehr humen race would hev sprung from thet mehn's loins. For goodness sake, thet would make him a relative of mhen.'

'And mine,' joined in Major Day with what sounded, for all the world, like a whimper.

'Yes, all of us would be able to trace our genes back to Ad-Im,' Doctor Hwy verified. There followed a moment's silence on the tape, only punctuated by sighs, groans and what sounded like a grown man crying.

The moment was brought back to earth by Allyson posing the question, 'Would that mean that he's to blame for my feet?'

'And the sins of the fathers shall be visited on the sons,' said Doctor Hwy, misquoting Exodus XX:5.

'But he's no' my father and I'm no' his son,' said Allyson misunderstanding the misquote.

Major Day tried to point out this inaccuracy to Allyson. 'You're taking it too literally, Miss Wonterland. It doesn't actually mean your father. It refers to the instructions Moses received from God or, as the Israelites called him, Yahweh.'

'I've never heard of Yahweh. Who's he when he's at

hame?' Allyson said.

Major Day persevered, 'The Israelites worshipped Yahweh. As I said before, Yahweh was what the Israelites called what we call God. In the Muslim faith, they worship Allah.'

'Oh, yes! I remember him – an awful nice man. He was worshipped right enough for a long time,' she said, wistfully. 'But then they all turned against him.'

'I think you'll find that the Muslim worshipers never turned against Allah,' assured Major Day.

'They did so,' Allyson said firmly.

'Are you sure you're talking about Allah. THE Allah. The same Allah, in whose honour, Saladin formed one of the mightiest armies the world has ever seen?' Major Day said, even more firmly.

'Yes. Allah. Allah McLeod. They all worshipped him – my father bought a living-room carpet purely on his say-so. In fact, he was in that very same army you were talkin' about. I remember him singin', "We're on the march wi' Allah's army". That's the same fellow and they did turn on him, by the way. I can assure you of that,' Allyson concluded, with the air of a woman who is sure of her facts.

'Eh wonder if we meht return to the epproximation of the truth, thet we were pessing off ehs reality, before we all got sedtrecked on the biggest load of old codswellop thet Eh hev heard in many eh day,' said Ewen Mee through, what sounded like, gritted teeth. 'You ken not seriously tell me thet any Supreme Being would choose Jolly ehs the mehn to kick stert humenity on Earth. The Bebl says God made us in his image. Look eht him,' shouted Mee, somewhat losing the plot. 'He is the most miserable looking mehn in the Western Hemisphere. He is eh full-grown mehn, who hes reached the age of meturity many eh year ehgo, ehnd yet still ken't make eh decision without consulting eh teddy bear thet he's convinced is his only real friend in the entehr world. For God's sake! He hes eh permanent drip at the end of his nose. Ehr you telling me thet God, Ehlleh, Yehweh, The Mester of the Entehr Cosmos hes eh bloody drip henging from the end of his NEB?'

'SHHH!' Doctor Hwy whispered. 'He's started talking again.'

END OF TRANSCRIPT

Thoughts are still whirring uncontrollably inside my head. I feel as if I am a man from another planet, who's from this planet that has been sent from this planet to the first planet and then sent back to this planet. I definitely feel that I have some previous knowledge of this place but I don't know what the knowledge is. A phrase is taking root in what's left of my brain. Eh! What is it I'm trying to? Wait a minute – yes, it is something along the lines of IN THE BEGINNING WAS THE WORD AND THE WORD WAS . . . What the hell was the word? What the hell is hell? I'm going to have to try and calm myself down and try to reconstruct . . . What? It's coming back to me, falling into place. Eh! I couldn't pay my tax so I've been sent here by . . . someone . . . what was his name? Oh, yes! Gord-On-Evan . . . to introduce mankind to this place by selecting one of the present inhabitants, mating with the said habitué and thus, hopefully, making one of them two of me. Then I can go back, promise to pay my Council Tax in the future and all will be well again. Basically, it's a conversion job. Shouldn't take too long.

Better try to take stock of the situation. I'll have a wee look round. Hmm! Well, quite a nice planet – could do with a dusting but, otherwise, not too bad. There is a large yellowy-orangey thing above me hanging on what seems to be a light blue thing that goes as far as my eyes can see. It hurts my eyes to look at it so I won't do that. Still at least it's warm – quite cosy, in fact. It feels a bit strange not having any clothes on. The dust is what I would describe as a very light-brownish colour and it seems to be all around me. In fact, it only stops at a large deeper-blue wet thing that eventually joins up with the light-blue thing that the yellowy-orangey thing is attached to. The wet thing makes a nice swooshy sound. It reminds me of what we call wet moisture on Alpha Sispens – except that I've never seen so much of it in the one place. On Alpha Sispens, it comes out of a syringe and has to have been treated before it is injected into us to keep us from drying up. I don't have an injection device with me so I'll have to try to figure some other way to stop myself from drying out. I notice, behind me, there are a lot of tall standing dark-brown things with green bits hanging from them. I'll have a look at them later.

Feel a bit stiff. I'll just stand up and have a wee bit of a stretch. AHHHH! That's better. Might as well have a walk down and investigate the dark-blue swooshy stuff. OHYAAAH! The light-brown dust is very burny on my feet. Just have to put up with it, I suppose, as I can't stay here for the rest of what's left of my time on Planet Dust – I mean Earth. Maybe if I run it won't be so sore. Here goes. OHYAAAAH . . . OHYAAAAAH . . . Here's the swooshy stuff coming up. OHYAAAA . . . OH! OH! HERE, THAT FEELS BETTER. The swooshy stuff feels nice and cool on my feet. I'll stay here away from the burny dust for a while. This IS nice. I feel very relaxed just standing here staring into the swooshy thing.

What's that? There are hundreds of silvery things in the swooshy thing dashing about between my feet. They're not actually touching me and, if I move my feet, somehow they manage to move with me but still without touching me. Maybe my feet are smelling. I must admit it's a while since I have been to the Alpha Sispens's cleaning regime programme. Anyway this feels very pleasant and not nearly as bad as I was led to believe from the Council.

I have been standing here for a long time and the big yellowy-orangey thing (I must try and think of an easier name than the big yellowy-orangey thing) is slipping down the light-blue thing (ditto for this) and I've also noticed that there is a lot of the light-brown dust at the bottom of the dark-blue swooshy thing. I am also getting a bit bored standing here so I am going to leave the swooshy thing, go back on to the brown burny dust and run up to the tall dark-brown things, with bits of green

hanging from them, to see what they are. Right. Here I go.
OHYAAAAH . . . OHYAAAAH . . . OHYAAAH . . .

That's me off the burny dust and now I'm standing on green
things that seem to be growing out of the brown burny dust. It
seems to me that the burny brown dust has green hair. I have
to say that my feet are sore, from not having my usual foot
guards on, so I'm going to have to figure out some way to
protect them.

After experimenting, I have discovered that the green things
that hang down from the tall dark-brown things protect my feet
from the burny dust if I wrap them round my feet and tie them
up with some of the burny dust's hair. This has allowed me to
go and explore Planet Earth further. It is much more colourful
than Alpha Sispens and, in a way, which I must admit took me
by surprise, it gives me an extremely pleasant feeling inside just
to look at all the things I've described. Apart from the creeping
crawling forms of life that the Council described, I have yet to
see any of the inhabitants of Planet Earth. I am also in need of
sustenance and fluid replenishment but have no idea how to go
about attending to these requirements.

A period of time has passed and there is something very strange
happening here. The big yellowy-orangey thing has slid right
down the light-blue thing and vanished into the dark-blue
swooshy thing. The light-blue thing has become dark blue, the
dark-blue swooshy thing has become black and a silvery-blue
round thing, very similar in shape to the previous yellowy-
orangey thing, is hanging up on the now dark-blue thing. This
has had the effect of altering the colours of everything. It has
also made strange sounds come from somewhere amongst the
tall dark-brown things with green bits hanging from them. I
have decided not to explore while the planet is black and blue
as I feel very uncertain of what to expect. The sounds are not
so much disconcerting as absolutely terrifying and instil a feeling

of uncertainty in me. One thing I am certain of is that some of these sounds are coming from the inhabitants of my new home.

I have discovered that the burny dust has been replaced by cold dust and all of the planet is now colder and more uncomfortable than it was when the big yellowy-orangey thing was up above. Trust me to land on the place just when its best days are behind it. This is a great shame as I actually felt good when I first got here. I quite liked the big yellowy-orangey thing even though it had not lasted long enough for me to give it a name. I am very tired but I'm frightened to close my eyes. I must try to think of something, anything, to take my mind off the ugly sounds coming from what seems to be all around me. Try to find a name for the big yellowy–orangey thing. Even though it's gone, it will make me feel good just thinking of it. If only I had been sent here earlier, then I could have enjoyed its feeling for longer. It has reminded me of when I was at the Alpha Sispens centre for learning and the good times I had with the friend that had been allotted to me by the Council. His name was Thisun-Izoot. So I decide to call the now departed yellowy-orangey thing Thisun-Izoot after him. They are both gone forever from my life so it seems appropriate. I am having great difficulty keeping my eyes open now. It's similar to how I feel when I need a service but I just had one before I got sent here – very puzzling.

I have just had the most awful, the most terrifying experience – the memory of which will never be erased from my mind. I am awakened from my state of tiredness by a sound that chills me to my bones. I witness a scene not twenty man lengths from me. One of the planet's inhabitants is being ingested by another one. On Alpha Sispens, we know, in theory, that this can happen. It is a very crude way to provide sustenance. Of course, no one ever actually does it as the whole process is considered barbaric. The Judicial Union of Nourishment Keepers (JUNK) provides food in the form of vitamin slabs. The slabs contain vitamins B,

E, R, Y and S and are collectively known as slabberys.

What I witness here is a virtual nightmare. I can only surmise that one of these inhabitants must have overpowered the other in some kind of strength contest. But, unlike the outcome of such an encounter at home where the victor would help the less fortunate combatant to their feet and treat them to a slabbery, here the unfortunate one who loses is ingested by the victor. It does not take long for me to figure out that I could easily be the ingested victim of such an encounter. My strategy, to avoid this happening, is to keep as quiet as possible and to shut my eyes and cover my ears so as not to have to witness the disgusting scene that is being enacted before me.

At long last, I open my eyes and, much to my relief, the carnage has ceased. I can see what I can only presume are the remains of the once hapless and now body-less victim. I am now, however, aware of the sensation inside my stomach turning from one of needing to empty it to one of needing to fill it by ingesting some slabberys. This is a huge problem because, unless I am way off the beam, I would imagine, from what I have recently witnessed, that this is a slabbery-free zone. Also, the inside of my mouth is extremely arid which is a sure sign that I am in dire need of wet moisture and, not only am I without the moisture, I am also without a syringe to apply it with. This predicament has given me a firm resolve always to pay my Council Tax in future.

At last, there's something to lift my spirits up – my friend Thisun-Izoot has reappeared. It seems to be rising upwards from the dark-blue swooshy thing and is climbing up the light-blue thing that goes on as far as my eyes can see. Also, the horrible noises in the middle of the tall dark-brown things with bits of green hanging from them have stopped. I notice that the cold brown dust is not cold any longer. With all these good things going on, I am determined to explore my new home further. Who knows? There may be some slabberys and some syringes lying about that I just haven't discovered. I am sure that, if I am successful in my mission to humanise this place, there will come a day when syringes will be lying about for anyone to use and JUNK food will be available for all.

Now that I can see a bit better, I decide to go further into the middle of the dark-brown things with green bits dangling from them. I am pretty far into these things when, suddenly, I come to a bit where there are no more of them. I am on top of a hill of some kind. I'm standing on a small flat piece of the burny dust's hair, that overhangs a large hole in the aforesaid burny dust, and, there below me, the most beautiful sight meets my eyes. What I see is a smaller version of the dark-blue swooshy thing.

It's stiller than the bigger version but its colour is the most startling thing about it. Never have I seen a colour that dazzled the eyes as this does. It shimmers with a green iridescence that even the Council chambers could not begin to emulate. As well as the colour, I notice something else quite remarkable about this wonder. It seems to have the tall brown things, with green bits dangling from them, growing upside down in it. But, after turning this over in my brain for a while, I realise that this amazing manifestation is not only unbelievably beautiful but it also has the power to reflect images – just like the image reflectors in Alpha Sispens. As I watch in awe and wonderment, I see something else that makes my heart leap inside me. Creatures of inestimable shapes and colours come to look at their images in the, the – what am I going to call it? What a dilemma? What a . . . ? What a . . . ? Oh! That'll do – I'll call it Wata.

As these creatures look down into the Wata, they create little circles in it and drops of the Wata gather round their mouths. They then proceed to lick the drops. After they have done this, they just leave the side of the Wata (or Wataside) and all of them go their different ways. I decide to try out what they are doing for myself, at some opportune moment, when I am more confident of my surroundings. It is while I am lying on the burny dust's green hair, trying to think of single words for all the new things I have discovered since coming to Planet Earth, that I make the next momentous discovery.

My stomach is beginning to ache, due to there being nothing of a slabbery nature inside it, when I see something that may just possibly save my life on this planet. I notice that, all around me, are round balls. They are orange, green, red, yellow, every colour I have ever seen and some I have never seen. Apart from noticing this, I give them no other thought until I see one of the inhabitants pick one up from the ground and chew on it in much the same way as I would chew on JUNK food back home. I begin to wonder if this could be Planet Earth's version of a slabbery?

There is only one way to find out. Reaching out my hand, I pick up one of the darker red balls and, before I can put it into my mouth, I experience another new perception. My nose is being assailed by such a sensation that my mouth starts to fill with moisture – but such copious amounts of moisture that I have never experienced before. I put my nose to the dark red ball and sniff at it. I have never done this before either as slabberys do not affect my nose in this way.

Before I can stop myself, I have put the ball into my mouth and I'm starting to chew on it. My mouth fills with liquid and pulp and the taste of it is such that I think I will pass out with the feelings of pleasure that are coursing through my body. There is a large hard bit in the middle that I can't chew but, otherwise, it is wondrous. I set about chewing on all the balls that make my nose make my mouth moisturise to the effect that my stomach is now feeling very full.

After a while lying on the burny dust's green hair, I notice a peculiar feeling inside my stomach. It feels as if it is growing bigger inside. The sensation is as if it is expanding due to some unseen force causing it to swell up inside. It is becoming extremely uncomfortable and I feel as if my bowels are going to explode. And, to my utter astonishment, that is exactly what happens. It begins with an irresistible impulse, inside my Exterior Rear Slabbery Evacuator (ERSE), to get rid of the swelling sensation. This leads me to deploy my ERSE into evacuate mode. To my astonishment, instead of the usual small pill-sized bit of waste slabbery being expelled from my system, I am party to my ERSE almost being rent asunder as something intangible but definitely vaporous erupts from within. The feeling of release is indescribable, as is the assault on the inside of my nose. I feel as though the lining of my nose has been stripped and, indeed, the lining of my ERSE is telling a not too dissimilar story. I cannot – dare not – move so I make my mind up just to lie there and finish off thinking of names for all the new things I have discovered about Planet Earth.

I am going to call the tall round dark brown things with green bits dangling TREES. That's T for tall, R for round and EE because that's the noise they make when they sway back and forward. Not ever having had to give names to anything before, I am finding it very difficult to go about using my new power of attorney. After a long time deliberating and listening to my ERSE (it's the first time it has ever spoken to me), I also decide to call the new things mostly after old friends I have left behind. This means that, every time I say the word, I will be reminded of them and it may help to fight off the inevitable homesickness I will experience.

I have, of course, already begun this process (probably subconsciously) when I called the big yellowy-orangey thing Thisun-Izoot after my old friend from the place of learning. So I am going to call the dust's green hair after the first female I was attracted to. She was, pretty, witty and very intelligent and her hair seemed to sway and smell not unlike the dust's hair.

Of course, she barely knew I was alive and she ignored me – indeed, she was the first in a long line of females who ignored me. Her name was Thigrass-Need-zcut. So, every time I trample on the hair of the dust, I will think of her.

Next up for me to give a name to is the light-blue thing that Thisun-Izoot hangs on. It seems to go on forever, filling up my vision and leaving no room for anything else above the dark-blue Wata. There was another friend at the Council centre for learning who, due to an over indulgence of slabberys, seemed to me to fill this description. His name was Thisky-Zil-imit so that will be the name of the light-blue thing.

I notice, while I am watching the silver-blue thing, which has taken the place of Thisun-Izoot, that it seems to have a large and expansive face – a face not unlike Thisky-Zil-imit's sister. She also had a passion for slabberys and her name was Thimoon-Izipal-holz.

Lastly, I have to find a name for the burny dust. An acquaintance, that I had almost forgotten, flashes up inside my brain – someone who, I think, could fill the need. He could never make his mind up as a student and was always torn between going one way or another – a bit like the dust when it swirls at times. His name was Thisand-That. It occurs to me that I don't need their second names so I'll just use their first names as I used to do back on Alpha Sispens. It will make it seem more friendly and informal as well.

I do miss having someone to talk to – someone to share and discuss everything that is happening to me with. At the moment, the only thing that is talking to me is my ERSE. It's not using actual words – that's true – but at least it's a human sound. I suppose it's my ERSE's language though it is me making the noise. Or, to put it another way, I am talking through my ERSE.

I have remained supine for a while now and, at last, my ERSE is silent and my stomach feels back to normal. There are no more creatures down at the Wata so I'm going to have a try at dipping my face into the Wata the way the creatures did. I have to make my way down carefully so I don't alert anything of my presence. I have spotted a way down and will start my descent after just one more vocal statement from my rear.

More joy – what a great time I am having! Eventually I get down besides the Wata's edge and, when I look into the Wata, I see my reflection. It is like running into an old friend. I wave to myself and almost faint with joy when I see myself wave back. Isn't it amazing that this simple act, which once I would have taken for granted, now makes my heart leap around and fills me with exultation. This, however, is not the end of my euphoria. I decide I will try to shake hands with myself. When I place my hand in the Wata, my whole reflection shimmers with a radiance that almost makes me weep. Never has anyone got so much pleasure from looking at me. Indeed, as far as I know, no one has ever got ANY pleasure from looking at me.

And still there are wonders waiting for my inquisitiveness. I just have to try what I had seen the various creatures do. Lowering my face, I gingerly dip it into the Wata. The sensation is one of shock. Never had I felt anything like it. I make a mistake that I will not make again. I have been taught a valuable lesson. The lesson is that I cannot breathe inside the Wata. When I hurriedly withdraw my face, there is Wata clinging to it. At first, I admit I panicked and tried to brush it off me but then I notice that, as I licked at my lips, this Wata has a cool and very pleasant taste. And I also find it is good to eat. This is a much more preferable way to ingest moisture than dispensing it into my arm with a syringe. I eat more of the Wata until I am quite satiated.

I feel very good and the tension of the past seems to drop from me. Thisun is high up in Thisky and there is a sensation of a cool feeling in the oxygen, which pleasures my body as it wafts over it. There is a moment of time on Alpha Sispens when the Council allows us humans to go to a place called Heed-En.

There we can do or say anything we want and there will be no repercussions. This moment is there to relieve us of all the stress that the Council gives us. It was introduced, many years ago, by a great leader that all the inhabitants of Alpha Sispens looked up to. His name was Kar-Ten and this time is known as Kar-Ten's Time. Heed-En was his birthplace. For us, that moment is the moment when we truly feel that life is good. This is such a moment. And it is at this instant that I decide to call this most wondrous of places after that great leader. From now on, I will be in the Kar-Ten of Heed-En.

I begin to feel that, if I have to stay here for longer than I had at first thought, then maybe it will not be such a hardship after all. This brings me back to my mission here on Earth. It also jogs a part of my memory that has remained, for want of a better word, unjogged – namely, I suppose I should set about finding one of these creatures I am supposed to reproduce with. It is not easy for me to see how I am going to accomplish this task. For one thing, I may not be what these creatures find desirable in a mate. And, even if I was, how would I know? It is certain that we will not be able to communicate verbally. So how do you say to someone who is not only not one of your acquaintances but not even the same species and, let's not forget, not even from the same planet, that you would like to begin a family? Could be tricky.

Of course, on Alpha Sispens this would be no problem. One merely takes whomever the Council has paired you with and puts her up for selection at the Department of Unborn Fertile Foetuses or, as we say on Alpha Sispens, puts her up the DUFF.

Another problem is where we are going to live. From what I can make out from my admittedly short reconnoitre, there seems to be a sad dearth of decent schools. How am I going to earn a living? I couldn't afford to pay my Council Tax on Alpha Sispens so what chance do I stand in this place. How will I even recognise my intended? From what I can remember, she will be swinging from a tree or picking at the skin of another of her species and then swallowing whatever she can dislodge from the epidermis. It's beginning to look as if perhaps the school situation won't be one of my major problems. I shall just have to tackle all these situations as they arise.

At least I feel good right now. Well almost! Thisun is starting to slide down Thisky and again this has the effect of making life feel not so pleasant on Planet Earth. I also notice that Thisky is not as blue all over as it was the last time. In fact, it is turning grey. And large dark lumps are gathering on it. I have a feeling that, like me, Thisky may have eaten too much of the round coloured balls because I can hear a distinct rumble coming from somewhere inside it – just like it did in me. There is another peculiar effect. Pieces of Wata are falling from Thisky and bouncing off me. The rumble from Thisky's ERSE is getting very loud and I can only hope that, if it does what mine did, the aroma is not index-linked as the lining of my nose will definitely not cope.

There is a noise like I have never heard before. It is so deafeningly loud that it makes the air crackle and spit and the Trees bend almost double and smash into each other. This has happened frighteningly quickly and has caught me totally unawares. I don't know what to do. Mechanically, I start to run – but where to? There is no escape from Thisky's anger. I have never had any experience like this back home which is where I wish I was now. Flashes of jagged light are striking the Thisand and making Thisand spiral upwards to join the black lumps that have now congealed to become an all encompassing darkness.

And then, in an instant, the dark is suddenly incandescent, splashed by a flash of brilliance that is truly terrifying in its power. The thought speeds through my brain that even the Council could not match this for scary moments. I am still running – blindly heading for I don't know what. In my panic,

I crash through green thing after green thing that seem to want to cling to me so I would take them with me to wherever I was going. I am so saturated with Wata that I feel I'll never have to moisturise again. I scream and shout with fear but I can't hear myself above the tumult that is going on around me.

Again Thisky lights up and, in the instant that the Earth is illuminated, I see an entrance in the side of a large rock formation. I don't know why but I head for it as if my life depends on it – which it probably does. The Wata is striking me so hard that I can't keep my eyes open and I grope unseeingly for the hole in the rock. My hands finally find it and I collapse through it. My breath is coming from me in great gasps but I feel that I am not in the immediate danger I was in a second ago.

I can't see anything inside the hole. Still at least I am no longer being assaulted by what I had previously felt was the friendly Wata. I am beginning to realise that, on Planet Earth, there is no such thing as a guarantee of complacency. Which is a shame because, where I come from, that is something you could be complacent about. Cautiously, I feel my way further into the hole. The sides are cold and slippery with moisture – not the most welcoming abode I have stayed in but I know I am safe from the dangers that are waiting outside.

I am utterly exhausted. Again I try to resuscitate from the back of my brain the word that I know will always, on saying it, rescue me from peril. What is it? I go back over the sentence. A word that will always, on saying . . . wait a minute . . . always, on . . . that is it. Is it? Something to do with alwayson . . . alwyson. I'm too tired. I'll try again after I have recharged myself. Alwys . . . Alys . . . Alyso . . . I can't remember – my eyes are heavy . . .

I've come to, still in the hole I sheltered in, but now it is flooded with light and there is a feeling of warmth in the surroundings.

Without looking, I instinctively know that Thisun has returned to Planet Earth. I'd better check anyway. Yes, I'm right. He is up there in his usual place and it is good to be alive again. I feel a bit in need of sustenance.

Once I have had a look round the hole, I will attend to that. The inside of the hole goes deeper into the rock than I first thought and is about three or four times higher than I am. I am going to see how far back it goes. Of course, once I leave the light of Thisun, it becomes increasingly darker. However, what I have decided to do is to keep going for as long as I can, until I can hardly see the light at the entrance, and then turn back.

I think I might just make up my mind to make this my permanent residence. It offers excellent shelter should I have another experience like the last one. It is now very dark and almost impossible to make anything out so I'll return to the front of the hole. When I step outside, the sight that greets my eyes is truly awesome. The Trees have all been flattened. The land looks like some giant foot has stood on it and destruction is everywhere I look.

On the bright side, lying around are plenty of the coloured balls which taste so good but make my ERSE do strange things. I notice that others are attached to the Trees and wonder if there is someone else on Planet Earth who is tying them on. Which reminds me of why I was sent here. From what I saw of the creatures in the Kar-Ten of Heed-En, there is no way I could pair off and make a go of it with one of them. They were all too fast for me to catch for one thing. Also, if memory serves me correctly, they all had no hands and five legs, one of which had no foot and protruded from the top of their ERSE. This one waggled about for no good reason that I could see.

Of course, they were eating the round balls that were lying on Thigrass and, if the effect on them was anything like it was on me, then the waggly leg was probably for waving the odour away. This is all, of course, conjecture and does not help solve

101

my immediate problem of making another human appear on the planet and helping out with the evolutionary sticking point or, as I've decided to name it, the evo-stick. Giving things a name is a great way to pass the time and I resolve to do more of it.

As I sit munching away at the round balls, I've just thought of a name for them. The noise that came from my ERSE was like FFFRROOOOT. So I am going to call the round and highly digestible balls Froot. I can also see that there are bits of Wata lying on the green things that dangle from the Trees. I don't know what to call the green things? They resemble the shape of a heart and are attached to all the Trees. I could call them hearts. No, I already have something called a heart. And so probably do all the creatures in the Kar-Ten of Heed-En. At the moment, I can't think what to call them. I'll leave them and come back to it.

I can hear a noise. From what I can judge, it does not appear to come from very far off. It is a crashing sound but not as loud as the noise I had to take flight from. I think I know what it is. It is the same noise my feet make when I am walking through Thigrass and stepping on the green things that have fallen off the Trees and are under my feet. The things that I haven't given a name to yet – the ones I said I would leave. That'll do – I'll call them Leaves. I edge my way out to get a better look at whatever is making the noise. I think concealment might be a good thing so I won't edge out too much. I can't see anything but I can still hear the sound of something crashing. It seems to come from above.

OH! MY! I can see it now. What am I saying, 'it'? There are well over a dozen of them. They are swinging from Tree to Tree and crashing through the green dangly things. By some miracle, they don't fall. I can see them very distinctly. They are covered in hair (as are all of the creatures I've seen so far). But there the resemblance ends. For a start, they have hands – hands that must be very powerful to be able to bear their weight as they

swing from the Trees. And their faces are not unlike my own –
except a lot uglier, of course. (Well, maybe not a LOT uglier.)
They have a body-shape very similar to mine except with
muscles. And, to confirm my worst fears, I have just witnessed
one of them picking at the skin of another one and then ingesting
whatever it found amongst the coarse brown matted hair that
covers its body. I say 'it' but I now know I should have said
'she' because, in what I hope is an unguarded moment, she
has decided to reward the picker by indulging in the act of
procreation. No! It's not an unguarded moment – another of
them is engaged in a similar act of thanksgiving. Oh dear!
They're all at it now.

What a cruel joke the Council has played on me. They
promised to dull my memory of how things are on Alpha
Sispens but they haven't and now I am able to contrast these
creatures with the humans I left behind and actually conjoin
with one of them in a bid to further their evolution or, to put
it another way, to stop the evo-stick. If I must bond with one of
them, I suppose I should make some effort to introduce myself
and try to become a part of their group.

As I watch them, I can see that even the little ones seem to be
– how can I put it? – at it. Dear me! I'll never keep up. On the
bright side, they do seem to get on with each other extremely
well. One of them has picked up a long thin yellow object,
which I have noticed hanging from the Trees, and is stripping
the skin off it to reveal another long white thing inside. He is
still actively engaged in carnal knowledge of a surprisingly
disinterested female companion and, for a moment, I am
extremely worried as to the use he was going to put the denuded
long yellow thing. To my relief and surprise, he is now ingesting
it with obvious enjoyment. I must remember that because I've
already tried ingesting one of these yellow things and didn't
like it. Perhaps my mistake was I didn't take off the yellow bit
first.

From my vantage point, I can see that an interesting development appears to be taking place. There seems to be something that has changed the mood of the group. They have stopped their group grope-athon and their mood looks to have changed from one of casual sex and informal ingestion to one of tension and anxiety. No longer are they in pairs but have formed themselves into tight little groups of three and four. The little ones are clinging to what I presume are their mothers. I can't see what is causing this dramatic change of mood but it is definitely prevalent in their behaviour. Happily they haven't spotted me. EHM! I think I've just been hit on the head by something and am about to pass out. Yes, that's right, I am about to . . .

TRANSCRIPT FROM THE JOLLY TAPES

The following is another record of what was going on
between Major Day, the Very Reverend Ewen Mee,
Allyson Wonterland and Doctor Has Kmee Hwy.

'Good God,' Major Day's voice was laced with strain.
'Will he be alright. Shouldn't we attempt to bring him
back?'

Allyson answered him in the negative, 'Naw, no' a
good idea. He's very deep inside his memory and the
jolt of being brought back involuntarily could maybe do
him permanent damage. He'll be fine. Did you notice
that bit where he said his feet were sore? I told you that
I had probably inherited my feet from him when he was
Adam.'

At this, the Very Reverend Ewen Mee jumped in. 'We
hev ebsolutely no proof thet Jolly was Edam. This is
only the ravings of ehn unbelenced mehnd under
hypnosis thet we ehr listening to. For goodness sake, his
mehnd isn't all thet belenced eht the best of tehms. This
is serving no useful purpose. We ehr, unless you hev all
forgotten, here to treh to fehnd out the possible
whereabouts of the Holy Grail. Ehnd listening to the
deranged ravings of someone who thinks they ehr
sodding Edem is not getting us any nearer to thet goal.
Eh epologehz for meh lenguage but really! Eh ehsk
you?'

'That's all right, Reverend Mee. We're all under a bit
of a strain and I'm sure that your use of strong
language is not all that foreign to most of us at times
like these,' said the Major. 'However I think we must go
by Miss Wonterland's advice as she is, along with
Doctor Hwy, the expert in her field. As you said

yourself, she has played The Pavilion Theatre.'

'Of course,' the Reverend Mee harrumphed, bowing to the Major's fierce logic, 'Eh got cerried ehway. Please eccept meh epology, Miss Wonterland.'

'Accepted,' was Allyson's curt retort.

'Is meh complimentery ticket for your next eppearence eht the Pevilion in jeopardy?' inquired Mee anxiously.

'Maybe,' was Allyson's shot across his bow.

Has Kmee Hwy cracked his knuckles as he solemnly intoned, 'I think it would be very wrong to bring him back. We are, I believe, at the very threshold of solving one of life's greatest mysteries. Charles Darwin's *Origin of Species* could only take us so far. I. M. Jolly has followed in his giant footsteps and supplied the answer to what even the incredible logic of Darwin could not solve. Darwin could only tell us of the origin of species – Jolly is showing us the origin of Man.'

'Utter tosh!' Mee was getting more and more agitated in his responses. 'If you expect me to believe thet menkind hes come ehbout because Jolly is ehbout to give way to some deep ehnd unmentionable desehr to prectise procreation with eh prehmate brought ehbout while under the influence of hypnotism, then Eh suggest you're off your trolley.'

At this, Hwy did go off his the trolley and leapt into the air before landing back on his feet and adopting the pose of an exponent of the martial arts. He made small whooping noises as he waved his hands in front of him and stood on one leg to stop him falling because his other one was measuring the distance between him and Ewen Mee's groin.

'You're just being silly now,' said Mee dismissively. This was followed by a squeal of pain as Hwy displayed that he was no slouch at measuring distances.

'What's he doing?' Allyson Wonterland asked, mystified by Hwy's whooping noises, waving fists and continual readjusting of the measurement from the end of his foot to the beginning of Mee's groin.

'I think it's Tae Kwan Do,' replied the Major, equally mystified at the turn of events.

'Take wan doo? Sounds like the beginning o' a recipe for pigeon pie,' Allyson said, maybe not grasping the exact accuracy of the Major's statement. 'Must be sore that,' she said, alluding, with total accuracy this time, to Ewen Mee's testicular tenderness. 'That's the way my feet get. It helps if I rub them vigorously. I don't think that's an option for the Reverend Mee though.'

The Major nodded in full agreement as he surveyed Mee rolling around the floor clutching his groin while, at the same time, trying to regain his facility for automatic breathing. Hwy was still hopping from foot to foot and whooping.

'Get him ehway,' Ewen Mee gasped. 'Eh thought Tibetans were supposed to be non-veholent?'

'Only the Buddhists,' whooped Hwy, smashing a chair to smithereens with the edge of his fist. 'The rest of us go berserk at the first sign of an insult.'

'I think an apology is in order, Mee,' said the Major, 'before the Church has to pay for any more damages to furniture.'

'Unless Eh hev missed something terribly important, Eh believe it was me thet was essaulted beh Jecky Chen there,' Mee said, in a very high pitched tone. 'Therefore, it is Eh who ehm deserving of ehn epology.'

'I would have to return to my village in disgrace if I apologised to a runt such as you,' Hwy replied.

'Who ehr you calling eh runt?' gasped Mee, gamely

rising to his full but unfortunately still tiny stature. 'Eh'm not ehfraid of you. Eh boxed for meh college. Like Mohetmeh Ehli, Eh could float like eh butterfly.'

Before he could continue the quote, Hwy interjected and said, with a whoop, 'Yes. You look like you sting like one as well.'

'Isn't it amazing that Jolly's slept right through all this?' Allyson cooed.

'Not really,' retorted the Major, getting between the combatants. One of them was standing on one leg, practising karate kicks, whooping and waving his hands in front of him. The other was standing on a chair and signalling the first one to 'Come ehead if you think you're big enough. You're not the only one who cen do kerioake, you know.'

The Major shouted as loud as he could, 'That is enough! In God's name no more.' Both Mee and Hwy, whilst still glaring at each other, dropped their fists. 'Kindly remember why we are here,' the Major continued.

At this point, there was a knock on the door and the voice of Shug the caretaker was heard from the other side of it. 'What's goin' oan in there?' he slurped, rattling the door handle. 'You're no' supposed to lock this door. I hope there's nothing funny goin' on in there that might force me to phone a newspaper and sell them a story aboot graft and corruption at a Church of Scotland yoghurt class? I hope yous are no indulgin' in any o' that sexual deviousness wi' her wi' the bad feet!'

'No everything's fine, thank you,' the Major shouted back.

'I'll need tae come in and see for maself. It's a condition of my employment that I have tae dae my nosy every so often, anyway,' was Shug's irritable response. The Major placed his finger to his lips in a gesture that meant hush. He whispered first to Has Kmee Hwy, 'Find a chair and sit down.' And then, to Ewen Mee, 'Stop standing on the chair and sit on it.' The two brawlers did as they were told and the Major moved to the door and opened it to reveal Shug.

He stuck his head into the room and slurped some tobacco juice from his suitably stained and singular top tooth. Suspiciously surveying the gathering, his eyes alighted on the broken chair. With a dubious shake of his head, he informed them, 'I'm no' acceptin' any responsibility for the fragility of the furniture. The woodworm can be fierce roon here. In fact, at the meeting o' the veterans o' the First World War last week, there was a sailor arrived wi' a wooden leg. By the time the meetin' broke up, he was a sailor withoot a wooden leg. So if yous are expectin' any compensation, yous are on to plums,' he advised. 'What's the matter wi' Holy Wullie oan the chair there? Has the yoghurt done him in?'

'If you are referring to the Reverend Jolly, he is meditating,' Major Day explained, almost truthfully.

Shug shook his head. 'I saw him when he first arrived and, if you were to ask me, it's no meditation it's medication he needs.' He then broke into a gurgling splurge-filled fit of what one would normally call coughing but, in Shug's case, was more like some form of deviant human lava erupting. Like a substandard building in an earthquake, his body shook while his lungs were rent asunder as he hung on to a wall for support. Finally, the thing that he used for a body stopped shaking and he announced that he was going for a smoke. 'Of course, if yous wanted to treat an old soldier to a tin of tobacco. That would probably mean I would have tae go to the shop for it and that would mean I might be away for anythin' up to a couple o' hours. This would mean yous could practise yoghurt tae your hearts' content and I wouldnae know nothin' aboot it.' He winked, with a leer playing round the brown stained trio of teeth that were floating in the saliva of the gap that he used as a mouth.

Major Day nodded in acquiescence that he could take a hint and gave him a suitable offering that would aid him in his pursuit of total expiration through tobacco.

As he was leaving, he lit up the sodden, soggy dog-end that was suitably stuck on his permanently moisture-laden lower lip and slurped. 'I see Holy Wullie's startin' tae come back to the land o' the livin'.' With that, Shug, the human swamp, took his leave of the company.

'Is he wakening up?' was the Major's anxious request to Allyson Wonterland.

'I don't think so,' she said after a brief study. 'I think he's still where he was when he said he was hit on the head. True his arms are flailing about but I think that might just be him reacting to whatever is goin' on in his regressive state. I wouldn't worry too much. If he gets into bother, he just has to say my name and he'll come out of it.'

'He seems to be trying to speak,' the Major said. 'Is there plenty of tape in the recorder? We don't want to miss anything because we've run out.'

'Eh hev eh spare tape recorder stending beh,' intoned Mee, 'though, if it is just going to be more of the same drivel, Eh'm beginning to think thet it's eh complete waste of tehm.'

'Shhh!' urged Doctor Has Kmee Hwy. 'He is starting to talk.'

'Don't you shush me,' replied Mee petulantly.

'You're being petulant again,' said Hwy, definitely stirring it.

'Oh! Shut up, the pair of you,' interjected the Major. 'He's starting to talk.'

END OF TRANSCRIPT

My head feels very sore and woozy. I appear to be lying down in some sort of clearing. I can't quite make the clearing out clearly as my eyes are not fully focusing yet. I'll try and rise up to a sitting position to see if that will help. Up we go. Ahh! That's a bit better. I can feel a large lump on the top of my head but I can't remember how it got there. I do remember dimly that I was watching something from some place of concealment. What was it? Something to do with why the Master, Gord-On-Evan, sent me to this place instead of L because L was too hot and full of things that could only crawl about the ground. I think that's about the gist of it.

There's something else. What was that again? Think Ad-Im think. Emmm – what was the reason I was sent here? Emmm – oh dear! I remember now. Unfortunately it's all coming back – only too clearly. I'm supposed to – I shudder at the mere thought of what I'm supposed to do. I can also remember what I was doing before I passed out. I was watching a group of swinging things. They were covered, for the most part, in hair – in fact, they were a bit like this group, sitting directly in front, that are staring at me intently whilst eating Gord-On-Evan-alone-knows what from each other's skin and playing openly with their – well, ehm, ehm – bits.

How I wish my eyes had stayed out of focus and I was blissfully unconscious again. There is a thud from just beside me. I have no idea what has caused it. Gingerly turning my head to try to assess what it is, I can see an oval, brown in colour and covered in hair. As I stare at it uncomprehendingly, I hear another thud. This time, I catch a glimpse of another brown hairy object as it falls from one of the Trees. The overtly over-sexed things seem to take no notice of them – well, that is, until now. One of the ovals has just fallen from one of the Trees and hits one of them on the head, causing it to keel over.

My brain begins to conjure with the possibility that this may have been the cause of the bump on my head and my subsequent retreat from consciousness. The rest of the group has taken no notice of their friend's fate – except that one of them has picked up the hairy oval thing and hurled it at me. Frantically, I duck as it whistles past my head and thuds into the Tree that I am propped up against. Terrified what might befall me, I squeeze my eyes tight shut. I know I can't run away as they would soon catch me. If I am to end it all here, then at least, with my eyes closed, I won't have to watch my own destruction.

My heart is pounding as I wait for the end. It almost leaps into my mouth when I feel my arm being tugged. Opening one eye, I tentatively look to where my arm is still being tugged and see one of the swinging things tugging at me with one hand while the other hand is holding up the brown oval that had slammed into the Tree behind my head. The oval thing has cracked and the hairy swinger is holding it up to its mouth. As it does so, I can see that some whitish Wata is dribbling from it and the hairy swinger is ingesting it. The swinger then hands it to me and grunts.

I am being urged to partake from the brown oval. Grasping it with both my hands, I hold it to my mouth and ingest the Wata. My doing this seems to excite the swinging things as they're all turning somersaults and running about screeching. The one who had offered the Wata pats me on the head and then proceeds to run about with its friends. I decide to join in and start screeching and running about too. This lasts for a couple of minutes and then they all settle down. My friend settles down beside me and starts to search my head with what is a surprisingly delicate touch. We are actually facing each other and my friend is going about the examination with an expression of rapt concentration that, I have to say, is quite endearing. Our eyes meet and then our foreheads touch. This act is one of tenderness and I feel somehow at ease with my newly found friend.

If, as I suspect, these are the creatures I have to kick-start evolution with on Planet Earth, then so be it. My friend Thisun is sliding down and turning Thisky from its various shades of light blue and white blue into a more even shade of slowly darkening blue. I shall call this the time of even-shade. And I shall call my new friend Eve-Sha to mark our first meeting. And, if we should produce offspring, he or she will be the first Council Approved Indigenous Newborn on Earth (CAIN). Accordingly, I will call the child CAIN and I shall teach CAIN mathematics and CAIN will go forth and multiply. And the next child may not be *able* to multiply or even add and subtract so I will call this child ABLE and ABLE will have to earn its keep somehow. So, if it's a boy child, he can tend sheep – whatever they are – and, if it's a girl child, she will have to learn to dance backwards. I am now going to become a swinger.

TRANSCRIPT FROM THE JOLLY TAPES

'Awww! Isn't that nice?' cooed Miss Wonterland. 'He's found the right wuman and they're goin' to live happy ever after.'

'NICE?' exploded the Very Reverend Mee, the veins of his neck popping with pent-up exasperation. 'HE IS EHBOUT TO COPULATE WITH EHN APE, FOR GOD'S SAKE!'

'Oh, calm down,' Miss Wonterland said, giving him a glance filled with scorn. 'Where's your sense of romance? You have to take happiness where you find it. And you'll definitely no' find it with a complimentary ticket for my next show at The Pavilion.'

Reverend Mee's eyes narrowed as he said, witheringly, 'If this is ehn exemple of your hendiwork, Eh wouldn't be in the audience for eh King's rensom. Eh meht fehnd myself rogering eh reindeer.'

'What reindeer would fancy you? It would have tae be desperate, so it would,' replied Allyson. 'And who would lift you up?'

'Et least Eh kehn enter eh room with out heving to take meh shoes off ehnd display the ugliest feet in Christendom. Fortunately they go very well with the rest of you.'

'THAT IS ENOUGH!' the Major barked. 'Will you both settle down? I have never seen such disgraceful behaviour since the last meeting of the United Nations. I want you both to apologise to each other – particularly you, Reverend Mee. Do not forget that you are a man of God.'

'Well, eccording to our tehm treveller there, Eh'm not – Eh'm eh mehn of GORD who, ehperently, is eh despetch worker on some fer flung gelexy called Elpha Sispens. Eh ehm sorry for meh loss of control but this whole thing is becoming preposterous.' With that he hauled himself up on to a chair and sat down.

As the tension-filled atmosphere pervaded the room, Has Kmee Hwy rose from his chair and paced back and forth, deep in thought. Finally, he spoke his thoughts out, to no one in particular, although the Reverend Mee probably suspected it was to him. 'You know this is maybe not so preposterous as you think,' he said, confirming Mee's suspicions. 'If Jolly, in a past life, really did come from another planet, he would not necessarily have to procreate with an ape. Depending on how far back he went, he might have arrived at the time of, for example, the Neanderthals. They were thought not to be ape-like but not human-like either. In other words, a perfect starting point for our friend here to kick-start the evolution to hominid. None of what he has revealed actually contradicts the existence of God. As I've said before, he is, in fact, remarkably, giving a logical explanation of the Old Testament.'

'I see where you are coming from,' the Major nodded, excitedly stabbing at the table with his finger. 'He said he had been sent here by Gord-On-Evan who was, as Mee says, a despatch man but he also said that there was a creator who did create us. The Master of Everything was how the description went. In Jolly's understandable confusion, he confused the two.'

'Exactly,' agreed Hwy, 'Gord-On-Evan obviously became God in Heaven over the years. Of course, Jolly being Jolly, confusion would be part of the package and would lead to all the various offshoots of polytheism that occurred before monotheism took over.' He noticed a look of total mystification on Miss Wonterland's face as she massaged her big toe. 'That is to say, the worship of many Gods rather than just the one God?' Miss Wonterland exchanged big toes but kept the look of mystification. 'Also, the name he gave to his friend – Eve-Sha – sounds not only like Eve but also his wife Ephesia.'

'Awww!' Allyson cooed again. 'Their love's endured through the ages. Isn't that lovely?'

'This gets progressively worse,' was Mee's response. 'It was behd enough being related to Jolly, now you're suggesting there's eh kinship with the wife. Hev you seen her?' He paused for further thought. 'Mend you, Eh kehn see where the Neanderthal tie-up comes in there.'

'Listen to George Clooney here,' Miss Wonterland said.

'Don't start all that again,' was the Major's constructive order. He surveyed both Mee and Miss Wonterland, ready to leap in at the first sign of dissent from either. Mee shifted huffily in his chair while Allyson tried, unsuccessfully, to stretch her twisted toes without the aid of her hands. Finding this well-nigh impossible, she inserted the fingers of her right hand in between the tangled toes of her left foot and just sat there, looking towards the ceiling and silently daring anyone (especially Mee) to comment. Wisely no one did.

'I think he's trying to come round,' Has Kmee Hwy announced.

'UNNNNHHHH!' was the clue to this deduction. It came from my still inert form slumped on the easy chair. 'UNNNHHHH! UNNNNHHH!' The inert form intoned.

'Eh see he hesn't lost his ebility to communicate fruitlessly with en audience.'

'Perhaps a drink of water might help?' the Major addressed the remark, urgently, to no one in particular.

'Or eh benena?' Mee responded, laconically.

'What shall we tell him has happened if he can't remember – eh – what has happened?' said the Major, uncharacteristically getting himself into a tangle.

'If only we hed eh photo of the wife ehnd weans playing in the Kar-Ten of Heed-En, Eh'm sure thet would jolt his memory,' added Mee, unhelpfully.

'You're not helping you know!' announced the Major before turning to Miss Wonterland. 'If I remember, you gave him instructions to remember everything, remember?'

Allyson nodded her head whilst unsuccessfully trying to extricate her fingers from between her toes. She thought hard before saying, 'I think it might be very difficult.'

'Bringing him back to the present?' asked Has Kmee Hwy.

'No! Getting my fingers out from between my toes,' she replied, irritably, still concentrating hard on the task in hand – and foot. 'If one of you could possibly help I'd be very grateful.'

'Ellow me,' said Mee, trying to ingratiate himself back into a free ticket for the Pavilion.

There followed an interval in the recording consisting mainly of me grunting, interspersed with Mee grunting as well. What was making me grunt was my efforts to extricate myself from deep hypnosis. What was making Mee grunt was his efforts to extricate Allyson's fingers from between her toes-es. Eventually, with the help of a fortuitous poker, which was found propped up against the wall next to the fireplace and was then used as a lever between Allyson's toes, the distressed digits were removed. Once the whitish tinge had disappeared and the feeling had returned to her fingers, Allyson returned to the question of my memory banks. The taped conversation continued thus.

'Although I asked him to remember everything that happened, that does not mean to say he definitely will. We are talking here about someone who has regressed to the beginning of time. Normally, they only go back to the First World War or the Jacobite rebellion. Mind you, the French revolution's getting very popular as well,' was her expert opinion.

'I don't think it matters as we have it all down on tape anyway,' Has Kmee Hwy said, stating the obvious.

'True enough,' agreed the Major. He then continued, disconsolately, 'This probably means the end of our grand adventure as Jolly will be in no fit state to continue. I'd like to thank you all for your efforts and – well – sorry we did not complete our task.' There was a murmur of concurrence from the group after which the Major guardedly asked, 'If, indeed, he doesn't remember any of what he has related, what do you think we should do if he – eh – asks about it?'

A silence signified that the answer to the Major's question was not an easy one.

Someone coughed. Then, after an additional pause, a disgruntled sigh escaped from between the lips of another. 'Hmmm!' came the sound of agreement to this.

'Hmmm!' another someone echoed.

'Well, I think we'll leave it at that then, shall we?' announced the Major, demonstrating true democracy at work.

'Eh think so.'

'As long as I don't have tae walk!'

'Hmmm!'

'Good.'

'I think he's trying to blow his nose,' Allyson informed everyone. 'We should maybe find him a hankie.'

'I'll give him mine,' volunteered Has Kmee Hwy.

'Better make it quick, Eh think he is going to sneeze. The sez of his nose he meht well envelop the lot of us in Wata,' Mee warned, sarcastically – but, as it turned out, too late.

'AAAAAAAtttttCHOOOOOOOOH!'

END OF TRANSCRIPT

I found my brain was still whirling as the noise of my sneezing made my eyes pop open – along with my sinuses. Looking back on it now, I can honestly say I had no idea where or even who I was at that moment.

'Welcome back, Jolly.' I could hear the Major's voice, dimly and indistinctly, though, at the time, I had no idea who it belonged to.

'Nice to see you back, Reverend,' said Miss Wonterland warmly.

'He hes bloody-well soaked me,' said Mee, damply.

'Can I get you anything?' Has Kmee Hwy asked.

'En unusually lerge bit of blotting paper would be comforting eht this precesse moment,' spluttered Mee, wiping himself down.

'I wasn't talking to you,' Hwy said irritably. 'Reverend Jolly, how are you feeling?'

'Where am I? Who am I? How am I?' The words still seemed not to be quite joined up with my mouth. It was like when the soundtrack is out of sync in a film. 'I feel as if I am in a film,' I heard myself say.

'The Plenit of the Apes?' I heard someone, who was probably Mee, reply.

'Was that Mee?' I asked.

'No, it was me,' said Mee confusingly.

'Yes, I thought it sounded like Mee.'

'No, it was definitely me,' Mee said, adding to my confusion.

'Is that Mee trying to confuse me?'

'He's definitely beck to his old self,' stated Mee, wringing out his necktie.

I could feel someone loosening my dog collar and the Major's voice comforting me. 'It's OK, Jolly, you're back with us. We'll get you a nice cup of tea and everything will seem a lot better. You're all right. Don't worry about a thing. Just relax. Would you like a cup or a mug?'

'A mug,' I said, weakly.

'Or helf eh coconut, perheps,' Mee chortled.

'I think that's enough from you, Mee,' said Hwy.

'Why?' questioned Mee.

'That's right, Mee,' answered Hwy, belligerently.

'Is that you, Mee?' I asked.

'Why?' Mee asked me.

'Is Mee annoying you?' Has Kmee Hwy asked me.

'Why ask me, Has Kmee Hwy?' I asked.

'All right, I'll ask you. Why?' Has Kmee Hwy asked me.

'Because I just prefer a mug,' I said, hoping to clear up the quandary.

A mug of tea was duly brought and everyone settled down. Gulping the first mouthful down my throat, I felt a sense of peace and belonging return to me. None of the others were speaking so I thought I would start the ball rolling. 'How did I do? Did we find the Holy Grail?'

'You mean you can't remember what happened while you were in regression?' the Major seemed to be a little bit concerned. His tone was that of someone uncertain of their position.

I hoped I could help him find himself. After all, as a Church of Scotland Minister, that's my job – solving people's personal problems and helping them on their way with an uplifting word of encouragement. 'Have you been up to no good then?' I enquired. 'You haven't found the Holy Grail and flogged it I hope,' I ventured waggishly.

The response was one of forced grins and reluctant grunts which, I must admit, was better than I usually got when I tried to be funny. Bolstered up with this reaction, I pursued my line of questioning. 'How near did I get? Did I find the Master? Do we know where the Grail is? Do we know WHAT the Grail is?' The questions tumbled from my lips thick and fast.

The answers, unfortunately, were thin and slow. 'Well, not quite,' said the Major, sipping thoughtfully at his tea. 'That is to say, you almost met the Master but . . .'

I'm afraid, in my excitement, I interrupted him, 'I almost met the Master? God in Heaven himself? Or is it herself? Is that why you're being so downbeat? It is isn't it? Well! Well! Mind you, I always suspected that he might be a woman. I mean why shouldn't a woman be the Master? Ephesia is certainly the master in my house. And look at how many female ministers there are in our Church these days. Of course, it'll be a bit of a blow for the Catholics – after all, they have consistently refused to recognise that women could be priests. Oh boy! They'll get it in the neck now. Not that we want to gloat about that but just wait till I see Father Daddi.' A thought struck me, 'I wish I had taken him up on the bet that God was a proddy. I knew it. Dear me, what odds would I have got that God was a *female* proddy? This could mean that all the priests will have to stop calling themselves Father and start calling themselves Mother.' I admit, at this point, I started to giggle uncontrollably. 'That will make Father Daddi Mammy Daddi.' It was while I was doing a little jig of joy that I was brought back down to earth (not for the first time that day) by the Major tugging at my sleeve and leading me back to my chair.

Seating me down, he proceeded to explain. 'I am sorry to spoil your flight of fancy but God is not a woman – at least not that we can prove,' he corrected hastily, as Allyson coughed pointedly.

'But you said I had almost met the Master, God in Heaven . . .'

This time he interrupted me, 'No, it was you who mentioned God in Heaven but, to be fair, you did connect with someone that – how shall I put it – sounded very close to God in Heaven.'

I gasped, 'Not, Peter, the Big Fisherman?'

'More like Gordon, the wee despetch mehn,' I heard Mee murmur.

'Shush it, Shorty,' warned Miss Wonterland, 'or it's more than your ticket that'll get punched at the Pavilion.'

123

'I don't understand. Did I or didn't I go back in time to try to find out what happened to the Holy Grail?' I questioned, taking all of them in as I glanced round the room.

Has Kmee Hwy was the one who responded first although the Reverend Mee was about to speak when, for some reason, the Major kicked him in the groin.

As Mee tenderly nursed his testicles, Hwy continued, 'You did go back in time but, unfortunately, you went – well,' he paused, 'a bit too far back.'

'You mean I went back to before Christ's time?'

'I'm afraid so. You are such a good subject for regression that you went way beyond what any of us expected.'

'Is that a fact?' I said, committing the sin of pride as I preened ever so slightly. 'Maybe I'll get it right the next time.'

At this, they all seemed to perk up more than a bit. 'Do you mean you would like to try again?' Hwy said, his eyebrows shooting up to his hairline while his jaw dropped below the collar of his polo neck in an extreme gesture of surprise.

Not being able to compete with this amazing feat of muscular dexterity, I could only say, 'If it's not too cheeky?'

They were all staring at me with inane grins on their faces. 'When?' was the next question from Hwy.

'Will after I finish my tea be alright?'

'This calls for a packet of custard creams, I think,' said the Major, beaming to everyone in the room, who all nodded in agreement and began to search for the money to put into the kitty.

'No!' the Major held up a hand to restrain us. 'This one's on me – or, should I say, the Church of Scotland expense account.'

We all laughed at his quip – I've no idea why – and Has Kmee Hwy reciprocated the Major's gesture by volunteering to go for the custard creams.

While he was out, I cornered the Major, 'Are you absolutely sure about God not being a woman?'

The Major shook his head, 'No, not really! It's quite possible that God might, indeed, be female,' he whispered. Then, glancing at Allyson Wonterland, he whispered again, 'They've taken over everything else so why not God as well, eh?'

I nodded and continued the whispering, 'Great, so I might still be able to call Father Daddi, Mammy Daddi?'

He nodded and we both shared a secret snigger. 'Fingers crossed?' he suggested. I suggested we interlock pinkies. He thought for a second then suggested we do both. To show him that I was not the type of man to jump into any decision hastily, I too paused for a moment's thought, then nodded in collusion. We both joined the pinkies of one hand while also crossing our fingers on our other hands. It was, I think, a moment that can only be shared by a certain type of man. I felt secure in the knowledge that my relationship with the Major had evolved into a deeper more masculine relationship. The only other person that I had a similar relationship with was Ephesia. However, Ephesia is always urging me to get more in touch with the feminine side of my personality. I've said repeatedly that I would if she would.

Has Kmee Hwy returned without the custard creams. Apparently, he said, they had sold out. The mood in the gathering at this news was sombre. However, after the initial dampening of spirits we all agreed with his choice of cheese footballs instead and gave him a group round of applause at his ability to take responsibility and make on the spot decisions. As we sat sipping our tea and eating our cheese footballs, there was a sense of optimism in the air – a feeling that nothing was beyond us, no problem was unsolvable as long as we tackled it together. Apart from Allyson's feet, of course. This feeling was, although modesty forbids me saying it, largely due to me. Nothing was actually said to confirm this but I knew anyway without having to be told. The mere fact that the biscuit tin had been placed directly in front of me spoke volumes. Being anxious to know what had happened while I was in my state of recession, I asked the company to relate to me the details. 'What kind of state was I actually in?'

'Eh hellova one,' was Mee's unhelpful reply.

I began to wonder if I should review my earlier conclusions regarding what a solid unit we had become when Allyson interrupted my train of thought by informing me that I had been in a regressive state.

'Like Russia was?' I replied, showing everyone that I was not just well versed in matters of the church but that I also had a firm grip on world affairs as well.

'No! Thet was eh repressive state,' said Mee, sticking his oar in where it wasn't wanted.

'Oh! That Russia!' I retorted, quickly covering up my slight error.

'Yes thet one – not the other one,' Mee intoned, studying me intently. He carried on intoning, 'What was the other Russia thet you were thinking of again?' laying a trap for me that I was not about to fall into.

'I was thinking of the one that has the very cold place in it. You know? What's it called? The place they send all the disinterested prisoners to?'

Mee surveyed me. He knew I had outmanured him. 'Eh think you meht mean dissident prisoners?'

I knew it was a last desperate throw of the dice on his part to outflank me. I was not to be outsmarted though. Quick as a flash, I was in, 'That's right – that's what I meant. What's that place where they're sent called again? I seem to have forgotten.'

'You mean Ehberia?' he asked with a mischievous smile playing at the corners of his mouth.

'The very place. I just couldn't remember the name of it,' I smiled, determined to be magnacartimus in victory. 'What Russia was it you were thinking of?'

'Same es you except mine hes SEHBERIA in it,' he said,

smugly, while, at the same time, removing the biscuit tin from in front of me.

Not to be out done, I rejoined the fray with, 'Is that the same as SIBERIA but just said with an imaginary bool in one's mooth.'

He was starting to lose the place as I recaptured the biscuit tin. 'Et least Eh hev never hed it ehway with eh fehr off prehmate,' was his strange reply.

I was up for it now though, 'You couldn't have it away with eh jehr of Coffee Mate,' I retorted, mimicking him. We were both now wrestling with the biscuit tin, aware that whoever it was that held the biscuit tin most probably held the balance of power within the group or maybe that was just me. By now, I didn't care – I just wanted that biscuit tin. Mee may have been Very Reverend while I was a mere Reverend but my dander was up and I was very angry. As we struggled, I became aware that Mee had actually stood up on the table to give himself the added advantage of the high ground. He was starting to use this advantage to its best effect when I remembered that he had been kicked in the testicles by the Major on another occasion. I also noticed that there was a cheese football just below his feet.

As he stood on it, I yelled, 'Oh, my goodness! One of your ghoolies has dropped on to the table. Watch you don't stand on it. AAAAAAAAAAHHHH. Too late! You've squashed it!' I screamed, pointing with my finger to the flattened football. 'It's stuck to the sole of your shoe.' With that, I pretended to pass out. Mee passed out with me – only he wasn't pretending.

As I lay on the floor in a pretend faint, I could see the others, out of the corner of my eye, gather round my inert body. The fact that they chose me rather than Mee made me appreciate that Mee was not as important as me to the current project. I wished Ephesia had been here to witness this rare occurrence. For some reason, I was usually the one who was always ignored so I knew that, without witnesses, I would never convince her that, for once, I was Mister Big.

I pretended to slowly come round, 'What happened?' I said, feigning weakness but noticing Mee coming round also. Waiting until he sat up and began to clear his head, I cried out weakly, 'Is Mee all right? Have they managed to sew his testicle back on again?' This had the desired effect of causing Mee to promptly pass out again. I could feel someone gently slapping me on the cheek with a hand. I assumed this to be Allyson as there was the odour of feet, mercifully faint, coming from the hand – either that or someone had stuck a cheese football up my nostril.

Allyson's voice cooed, 'What a nice man. Even though he's passed out himself, his concern is for that wee weasel lying at the back of us. That's showin' real Christian spirit, so it is.'

At this, I heard the Major say, 'Good grief, I forgot all about Mee.'

Realising I was about to forfeit being the centre of attention, I rose up just as they were about to turn round and attend to Mee. 'Attend to me first,' I said.

Has Kmee Hwy replied, 'Of course, we are just seeing to him now.'

'No! Not Mee – me,' I demanded, maybe losing the weakness angle slightly.

'Don't worry. We are doing everything we can for him. You just lie there and try not to fret too much for Mee. He'll be fine,' assured Has Kmee Hwy.

'I'm not fretting for Mee – I'm fretting for me!' I shouted. I was now possibly verging on full-blown petulance but I found it impossible to draw back from this precipice of peevishness. 'Leave Mee alone and see to me,' I yelled.

'The man's capacity for self-sacrifice is awesome,' said the Major, rubbing Mee's hand with his own. 'After all he's been through, he is still more concerned for his fellow man than he is for himself.'

At this, I admit all restraint left me and I started screaming. 'Will you listen? I want you to attend to me – OK? Me, me, me!

I don't give a flying fig about Mee. I want you to leave Mee and concentrate on me. Love me. Love me. Love me.' I admit I had now lost it completely but it felt good.

The last thing I remember was Has Kmee Hwy applying a finger to the side of my neck before I vanished into oblivion.

When I came round, the Very Reverend Mee was stroking my forehead. I gave a little involuntary jump. Mee's voice had a strangely soothing and kind tone about it. 'It's all reht, old chep,' I heard him cajole. 'Eh heard from the others of your selfless concern for meh well-being. Rest essured, you hev found eh friend not only in Jesus but also in me ehs well. Would you lek eh wee cup of tea perheps?' I nodded to him that I would, indeed, like that and, laying my head gently back on the floor, he announced, 'Eh say, everyone, look, our old pell Jolly is beck among us. Will someone ettend to his needs while Eh make him eh wee cup of tea?' I was helped carefully on to a seat at the table by the other three while Mee put on the kettle.

'Sorry about putting you to sleep but you were in danger of exploding with a generosity of spirit that we see all too little of these days,' Hwy's hand rested gently on my shoulder as he apologised for knocking me out. 'I hope I'm forgiven,' he pressed, thankfully with his voice and not his hand. 'Can I get you a biscuit?' I nodded again. 'Good. Man can not live by bread alone, eh?' he quoted as he passed the biscuit tin still containing only cheese footballs.

The Major leaned towards me from across the table, 'Rest assured, Jolly, I will be bringing your extraordinary act of selflessness to the attention of the Moderator. Piety, such as yours, deserves to be recognised and, indeed, paraded in front of as many people as is possible. Oh, I know you'll probably balk at the notion of being praised to the heavens and want to remain anonymous and take no credit for being the exemplary human being that you are. I can just see you refusing all the benefits that will probably be thrown at you, eh?' he smiled.

I began to panic a bit, 'Well, maybe not. I'll maybe accept one or two of them – just so as not to appear rude. I've always felt rudeness was a terrible sin – maybe even worse than the sin of eh . . . of eh . . . avaricitisness.'

The Major's brows knitted together in thought. 'I've never heard of that one.'

I leapt in, 'Oh, it's quite a bad one – not, I admit, generally known but it's definitely there, all right. It's up there with the sin of eh . . . of eh . . . slothithity.' I could see all their brows starting to knit. 'Anyway,' I careered on with a deft change of subject. 'Let's not dwell on me and any rewards which might be coming to me. What about the next step in our quest for the Holy Grail?'

The Very Reverend Mee placed a mug of tea in front of me as Major Day gave me the thumbs up from the other side of the table. 'That's the spirit.' And they all began to sing 'FOR HE'S A JOLLY GOOD FELLOW'. I smiled shyly and shook my head modestly as I held up my hands for them to stop while, at the same time, stamping my feet under the table so they would stay in time. When they finally came to the end, everyone stood up and applauded – including me. I admit I thought I'd blown it, when I got carried away with it all and applauded myself, but they all thought that I was being self-effacing again and was actually applauding them. As the saying goes, 'What's for you will not go by you'.

Major Day began to relate what had happened in my last attempt to track down the Holy Grail. He did not go into detail but told me that I had gone back just a weenie bit too far and had narrowly missed the target. Has Kmee Hwy asked Miss Wonterland if, the next time she put me under, maybe she could suggest a background to the period I was intended to visit. This would act like a sort of signpost to direct me in the general direction I should be heading. Allyson agreed that, although there were no guarantees, it did offer up possibilities for an approximate, if not exact, hit.

We all agreed that we would have another go after we had had one more cup of tea and a suitable toilet break. As we prepared for my next venture into the past, the mood in the room was one of nervous tension – this was probably because I was nervous and the rest were tense. This tension did not, however, seem to stretch to the wonderful Miss Wonterland who, by now, was on her fourth cup of tea. As she sat reading a copy of that month's *Podiatry for All*, she was a picture of calm unruffled tranquillity. Only the manifold crumbs of long digested cheese footballs, clinging to her polyester pullover, betrayed the inner passions and appetites she must have had in order to be able to keep a Saturday afternoon matinee audience at the Pavilion satiated. She was oblivious to everything that was going on around her, all her focus being concentrated on the magazine's top feature – 'Celebrity Corns'. This apparently comprised of various photographs of celebrities' corns. The only thing that ended her concentration was when her face broke into a wide beam as she announced to us that she had finally matched her corn to a celebrity one. We all felt sad for her when she found out it was Giles Brandreth's. No one spoke as an air of embarrassment replaced the air of nervous tension. However, like the trouper she undoubtedly was, she picked herself up from this awful revelation and, symbolically brushing off the old crumbs from her pullover and popping a brand new cheese football into her mouth, she announced she was ready to start the proceedings.

Major Day ushered me to my easy chair and, while Mee pulled the curtains and checked that the door was locked to prevent any unwanted intrusion by Shug (actually, I don't think there could be a wanted intrusion by Shug), the scene was set for the next attempt at finding the Holy Grail. The Major addressed Miss Wonterland, 'Now then, Miss Wonterland, could you, as doctor Hwy suggested, perhaps implant, in Jolly's mind, a few more precise facts that may help him to zero in, a bit more accurately than the last time, on the period of history we are aiming for?'

Has Kmee Hwy continued on this theme, 'For example, if you can get Jolly to concentrate hard on certain historical facts, then some of his long-dormant memory cells may, with luck, kick in and place him at the precise spot in history in which we are all interested. In Tibet, we call it "Astral Travel".'

Mee piped up, 'Everywhere else it's called "Eh Load of Twaddle".'

The Major rounded on him. 'Don't start!' he commanded.

'Eh didn't mean Eh thought it was eh load of twaddle,' Mee replied defensively. 'Eh was merely commenting on how the rest of the plenit viewed the phenomenon.' He was rapidly heading into huffy mode again. 'Honestly, it'll get so you kehn't speak shortly.'

The Major defused this potential flash point by saying, 'Well, why don't Mee and me fill in the religious details and Miss Wonterland can supply the historical details?'

Miss Wonterland declined this by informing the meeting, 'I don't know anything aboot history. Why can't Hwy do the history bit?'

Doctor Hwy nodded, 'I have no problem with that. The period in question is between BC and AD and . . .'

Mee held up his hand. 'Permission to speak?' he droned, sarcastically.

Major Day was not best pleased as he told Mee not to be childish and that of course he could speak.

'Eh was just checking for clerification,' Mee explained, pointedly. 'It's just thet it hez occurred to me thet the presumebly dorment nodules in Jolly's noddle will not recognez the terms BC ehnd AD because they were not extent eht thet perticuler moment in history. Or is thet me just being cheldish ehgen?'

There was a long drawn-out pause, only broken by a small

grunt of satisfaction from Mee, before the Major spoke. 'Reverend Mee is right, of course. This could mean the end of our quest. We can't just keep sending Jolly at random into the past – it's far too hit and miss. It looks like we are at an impasse.' An air of despondency that was both swift and heavy pervaded the room. Even Mee seemed to take no pleasure in the fact that his blinding logic had put the Peter on the project.

However, I was not about to let my dreams of perhaps meeting the man I had dedicated my life's (make that lives') work to. There was also the small matter of bringing my beloved Church of Scotland to the forefront of ecclesiastical eminence and, last but not least, my getting to meet my hero – The Moderator of the General Assembly of the Church of Scotland, or, as he's called for short, TMOTGAOTCOS. 'What if you just suggested to me things that were going on at around that time? For example, the Romans ruling the Christians . . .'

Doctor Hwy interrupted my flow. 'Jews,' he stated.

'Jesus was a Christian,' I pointed out.

Hwy spoke again, 'At that time he was a Jew.'

I have to say I found his splitting of hairs quite irritating. 'Can we settle for a Christian Jew?' I said, hoping he would pick up on the note of impatience in my voice.

'I suppose we'll have to,' was the not too enthusiastic response.

I carried on regardless, 'If I concentrate on the despotic Roman Empire persecuting Jewish Christians in the Far East . . .'

'Middle East,' Hwy annoyingly interrupted again.

I went along with it, however, or we would have been there all night. 'All right – Middle East. I'll begin again. If we concentrate on a despotic Roman Empire persecuting Jewish Christians in the Middle East who are led by Jesus Christ can we . . .'

'His second name was not Christ,' Hwy's flat tones again stopped my proposed plan. 'That comes from the Greek word

Chrissos meaning "Saviour" and was not applied to him until Paul went to Greece and converted the Corinthians. Nor was his name Jesus – Jesus is Latin and comes from the Greek for Joshua. In fact, he was probably known as "Joshua bar Joseph".'

'Did he have a pub?' I asked, incredulously.

'No,' Hwy replied, equally incredulously. 'His father was Joseph. *Bar* means "son of" – therefore, he would have been "Joshua bar Joseph".'

There was another long pause as I stared at him before caustically enquiring, 'Are you going to keep this up? Because, if you are, we'll be here all night?'

Before Hwy could answer, Major Day leapt in, 'My dear Jolly, suffice it to say, if you feel that it is within the bounds of possibility for you to bring our quest to a successful conclusion and despite the risks involved are willing to give it another shot, then it ill-behoves us to deny your selfless offer. Are you offering?'

'I'm offering.'

'Then we're accepting.'

Everyone applauded again and once more they sang 'FOR HE'S A JOLLY GOOD FELLOW'. This time I didn't join in as they would have noticed my feet tapping but, when they had stopped, I made an observation that I felt was pertinent. 'I would like to make a suggestion,' I said. 'I fully take the point that the Very Reverend Mee has made about my not being aware that I would not be aware what BC, etc. meant if I was actually living during those times.' Mee nodded graciously. 'Because,' I carried on, 'obviously the calendar would have been different due to the fact that no one was aware that a humble carpenter's apprentice from Galilee would become the Saviour of the world.' Everyone nodded in accordance with this. 'And even those who were aware would be wary of letting on that they were aware in case someone found out where the wary aware were and they got a doing.'

Everyone shook their heads. My logic had obviously caught them unawares. 'Anyway, what I am suggesting is that, despite all that, I would like Miss Wonterland to plant in my brain, during the first bit of recessing me, the fact that I should concentrate on those dates because I am comfortable with thinking in those terms and it might just help to focal me in on the era in question.'

The Major nodded and rubbed his chin thoughtfully. 'Are you trying to tell us that you would like to begin with the modern way of dating time and then, as you go further into regression, we suggest only the pertinent happenings?'

It was my turn to nod so I did. 'Yes, I am very at home with that system – indeed, I formulated an improvement on it which you may like to hear?' It was their turn to nod but strangely only Major Day did. 'Well, instead of the normal BC and AD, I start with LBC, then ABBC. Then I go to BBC, JBBC, CIA, ABC, then DC, then AC.'

Mee's face was grim as he tried to follow my system. 'Eh know Eh should not go down this route but Eh ken't help mehself. So, what does all thet mean?'

I explained thus, 'LBC is "LONG BEFORE CHRIST". ABBBC is "A BIT BEFORE BIRTH of CHRIST". BBC is "BEFORE BIRTH of CHRIST". JBBC is "JUST BEFORE BIRTH of CHRIST",' I paused, noting the looks of astonishment on all their faces. Except, of course, Allyson's. She had gone back to her podiatry magazine.

'CIA?' asked Major Day, in what can only be described as wide-eyed astonishment.

'"CHRIST IS ALIVE",' I explained, glad that he was so amazed by my logical logistics. 'ABC is "AFTER BIRTH of CHRIST". Then DC is "DURING CHRIST". And AC is, of course, "AFTER CRUCIFIXION". I think you'll agree that it makes that era so much more understandable. That is why I would like Miss Wonterland to suggest these dates to help me when I become comatose.'

'Ehn excellent suggestion,' said Mee. 'Eh was certainly cometesed listening to you – specially the bit about Christ's efterbirth and the AC/DC period of his life. Eh think you ehr on to eh winner there, Jolly.'

I could tell Major Day was not quite so enthusiastic by the withering look he drew Mee. He stared at me for a moment, shook his head twice and said, 'If you think it will help, then by all means continue to think along those lines, Jolly. If I could ask you to just keep those dates to yourself as I'm sure you will appreciate that Miss Wonterland may have some – how can I put it – initial difficulty trying to remember the – eh – initials!'

I signified that I understood by rather wittily replying, 'OK.'

Major Day seemed unduly relieved – if not at all amused – and suggested that we begin. Allyson was informed we were ready for her and, laying aside her copy of *Podiatry for All*, she settled down at the side of my chair. I could hear the barely audible click of the tape recorder being switched on before Allyson began to speak in that incredibly soft and reassuring way that made me relax into myself. She again told me that she had studied the tea leaves in my teacup and that they were very favourable. I could feel myself starting to drift as I recited LBC, ABBBC, BBC, JBBC, CIA, ABC, DC, AC and then back to the beginning to start all over again. It was a bit like counting sheep except for the fact that there were no sheep. I could also hear that I was being reminded about the conditions of the time I was trying to zero in on.

Allyson's voice reminded me that I only had to call her name out loud and I would return safe to the present day and, therefore, I was not to have any anxious thoughts. I just had to concentrate on the wonderful feeling of drifting about in my mind and my memory banks.

Hwy's voice kept invading my reverie by reminding me about the conditions and politics of the time. Suspicion and intrigue were rife, apparently, and the doctrine of Christianity was very new, blah, blah. I could hardly hear what he was saying now. JBBC, CIA, ABC, DC, AC. ABBBCC, JBBCCACD-CCIA, BOAC, CO-OP, BBCCZZZZZZ.

I can feel the heat of the midday sun pervade my little room as I have my usual afternoon nap. I have always been very fond of this time of the day. It is the period when all men can throw aside their worries, close their eyes and be alone with their dreams. And who can dream better than I – I, Julius Jollius, soothsayer to the nobility. Once I have closed up my consulting chamber, then no one will disturb me. No one – not even the highest born of Rome's citizens – because they too have all fallen into the arms of Morpheus. The Greeks were very generous to share their God of sleep with us Romans. However, it would only be good mannered of us to invest in a God of sleep of our own and not put such a heavy workload on poor old Morpheus – after all he may get tired and fall asleep. I smile inwardly at my jest.

What should a Roman call a God of sleep? I stretch out luxuriously and continue in my muse. It would almost certainly be feline as nothing can stretch as well as a cat. That might be it – the Goddess Catnap and her even sleepier husband the God Catatonic. What a civilised invention this afternoon nap is I chuckle silently. Truly the man who first dreamed it up should have been awarded a consulship or a triumphal walk through the streets while garlands of flowers were strewn beneath his feet. Lying outstretched with nothing to do all afternoon, I think of the words of the poet Virgil, 'Time flies like an arrow but fruit flies like fruit.' And what a complete bum wipe he was.

My mind luxuriates on the sheer bliss of not having to say a sooth for at least the next hour or two. The morning surgery had been very profitable and I had successfully advised four very wealthy and very gullible clients. It never ceases to amaze me that, when I ask, 'What can I do for you today?', they never think that, if I could really see into the future, then I would know why they were there and what I could do for them.

The last client of the morning – an exceedingly ugly old patron – asked if he would ever find a woman of wisdom and beauty to share his life with? I told him 'Yes, Incubus Trolleybus! First you must find a beautiful young woman. Having satisfied that first part of your quest, you must then ask her if she would rather marry a rich old man – such as your illustrious self – who will ply her with gifts and also make her the mistress of a large house with lots of slaves to look after her every whim, until the day he dies, or a handsome young drunkard who would not be able to look after her because he would be too busy looking after every other woman who passed by. Sooner or later one of them will select the first option and you will have found a woman with beauty and the wisdom you seek. I forecast sooner rather than later.'

The silly old duffer went off minus thirty gold coins and promising me a further bonus when he found his heart's desire. I forecast that he will be back this evening at the latest. A voice cuts through my musings. It is such a voice as could bring the birds down from the trees. Birds do that when they are stunned.

'Julius Jollius?' it booms, sending shivers through every living creature in the house. 'I hope you are not lazing about when I have things for you to do. The emperor has sent a barrel of wine for testing, in case it's poisoned, and he wants it back by tonight. They're having another orgy at the palace and they've run out of toxin tasters. They want you to foretell if anyone will snuff it.'

It is, of course, my wife Ephesa Excreta, the daughter of the crap merchant Ephesius Excretius. He had been a scrap merchant but the bottom fell out of scrap and he turned to crap. Roman tradition meant that the daughter took the father's name.

However, it always ended in the feminine letter (a) rather than the masculine (ius). Ephesa had only one friend. She was the daughter of the senator Watius Vulvius. This, of course, gave an unfortunate slant to her name. Being that rare thing in Roman society – blonde – Watta Vulva was always much sought after. There is a popular misconception that blondes are somewhat gullible and cheap jokes are always being made about them. The latest one being 'How do you get a blonde to marry you? . . . Tell her she's pregnant.' I wonder if Incubus Trolleybus has heard that one – if not, I'll send him after a blonde this evening. However, as far as Watta is concerned, strangely, mister Rightius remains inconspicuous by his absentious. She absolutely worships Ephesa and defers to her as if she were a veritable Goddess – indeed, we all defer to Ephesa, eventually.

She is very busy at the moment preparing for a meeting this evening with a gathering of overbearing females, known locally as 'The Prominent Dominants'. They are going to be discussing the problems of being a matriarch as regards the management of domiciles, rodent problems, lice on the rodents and husbands in the domiciles, in that order of importance. Ephesa is giving the meeting a lecture on this subject in her capacity as chairwoman of the HOUSES, MOUSES, LOUSES AND SPOUSES SOCIETY. Consequently, I am in hiding in case I'm called upon to volunteer (I use the term loosely) as a life model for the mouse part of the lecture.

Her voice rings out again, scattering a flock of sheep that happen to be passing the front door. I can hear the herdsman trying to round them up by barking as if he were a dog. Times are so hard in modern-day Rome, with the punishing taxes imposed by the mad emperor Gaius Caligula, that he obviously can't afford to keep a real dog. If he had come to me for advice, I would have suggested that he kept the dog and got rid of the sheep – cheaper in the long run. 'Julius Jollius!' I can feel her words flay me, like the lash on an old slave's back. 'You'd better not be listening to me and pretending not to hear. Answer me. Where are you?' She bellows.

A stunned sparrow falls on to the ground just in front of my hideaway. As it gets up and groggily tries to walk about, I decide, for the sake of the local wildlife, to answer her. 'I'm here, my little cactus plant. Were you wanting me for anything special?' I try to erase the note of trepidation I invariably feel when I speak to Ephesa but, try as I might, a quaver unites with the trepidatious note and, as usual, my voice comes out like one of the sheep that had been scattered a moment ago.

'Stop bleating,' she commands as the ground shakes in response to her descending the stairway. 'Mice don't bleat, they squeal and that's what you'll be doing if you don't test the barrel of wine that Emperor Caligula has sent round for veri-fication of its toxicity.' Her eyes alight on mine and I feel that old rat in the gaze of a cobra syndrome.

'I see. I'll test it thoroughly and make sure it's free from poison before I send it back, light of my life.'

Her gaze strengthens its hold on me, the yellow of her eyes (Yes, that's right – yellow.) transfixing me. 'Are you totally off your toga? It's not supposed to be free from poison – the emperor wants you to make sure it's poisonous enough.'

'Of course, it's August,' I remember, trying unsuccessfully to blink.

'That's right and what is August?' she says, talking to me like a child.

'It's the emperor's Poison a Pal for Piety month.'

She gives me a wearisome look of impatience. 'Correct. Last year it was Crucify a Crony for Caligula month. But, this year, he is concerned that we'll all be bored and think him unimaginative so he's changed it. Next year, it will hopefully be Jettison Jollius in June, for Jove's sake. Until that happy time, get testing.' Her gaze sweeps away from me and alights on the ground to the left of her. 'Why is that sparrow staggering

ONE DEITY AT A TIME. . .

around with its wings over its head?' she asks accusingly as if I had especially requested the bird to annoy her by doing this.

'I can't think, my little ache in the anus,' I answer.

'What did you call me?' her voice thunders. I never knew sparrows could cross their eyes until that moment.

I am so taken aback by this phenomenon that I nearly forget to lie through my teeth as I answer, 'I called you my little Akinaennuss. Akinaennus is, as you probably have heard, sweetness, an Egyptian Goddess of unassailable beauty and wisdom.' This is enough to get me off the hook as Ephesa is neither up on Egyptian deities nor averse to a little flattery. This being the case, I never take any chances and always go right over the top in the cause of self-preservation. As Virgil says, 'If two wrongs don't make a right, try a third one.' But then we all know what a natural nipple he could be – the only man in Rome who could strut sitting down.

'Where is the barrel in question, dearest?' I ask.

'In the yard, of course,' she rasps in response. 'Have you noticed? That bird's eyes are crossed,' she continues.

'Which bird is that, my little bee sting?' I enquire.

'I've just told you,' she yells. 'The one with the crossed eyes. Have you been sacrificing to the Gods of dimwits again? How many times do I have to repeat myself. Could you possibly try to concentrate for just over a second?' Her vast bulk shakes with displeasure, causing currents of air to emanate and the leaves in the viburnum to rustle in the wind that flows from the bumps and lumps she uses instead of a body. 'It may just make my life with you a tiny bit more bearable or, better still, have a cupful of Caligula's wine – with any luck that could make my life infinitely more bearable.'

Mercifully, she sweeps off, leaving me and my cross-eyed friend to revel in the peace and tranquillity that settles in her wake. I pick up the poor little mite and examine its ears for signs of blood escaping due to punctured eardrum syndrome.

I give up, however, when I can't find its ears. For a moment I wonder whether Ephesa's voice has actually blown them off. Then I muse that I had never seen a sparrow with ears.

As I wander through to the courtyard and the emperor's barrel of vino collapso (literally), I realise that, in fact, I have never seen any kind of a bird with ears. How do they hear? As I examine my little friend again I notice that its eyes are beginning to uncross. A small frightened chirp escapes from its beak. Not wishing to add to its fears, I open my hand and watch my new little friend as it soars away, dipping and diving to freedom and the pursuit of happiness and then crashing into a lone poplar. (Maybe I should have waited until its eyes had fully uncrossed before I released it.) The barrel of intoxicating toxicant that is awaiting my forecast as to its capacity to turn a consul to a corpse squats silent and sinister in the sunlight.

Our dear emperor Gaius Caligula is, of course, as mad as a March hare. He has recently returned from supposedly conquering Germany. He didn't even see a German never mind conquer one. And, apparently, so the tales in the marketplace go, he blamed Neptune, God of the sea, for making the waves so high that he got seasick and was forced to turn back. He then challenged Neptune to single combat. Surprisingly enough, Neptune did not respond and our illustrious emperor, therefore, declared war on Neptune and raided the God's treasure trove (You couldn't make it up could you?) to pay for the cost of his German campaign.

On returning to Rome, he displayed his plunder for all to marvel at. The plunder consisted of five thousand chests stuffed with seashells, two thousand tons of seaweed, one hundred and fifty boxes of sand, ten mackerels, seven sardines and a bag of whelks. Not surprisingly, there was not a spontaneous round of applause from the great and the good of Rome. This show of indifference put him into a fearful temper and he has been taking it out on the populace ever since. Poisoning his pals is his latest hobby and he brags to anyone who will listen that he learned the art of the poisoner from his mother, who learned it from her mother, who learned it from her mother, etcetera, etcetera. Etcetera Etcetera was her name, being the daughter of her father, Etceterius Etceterius, a valiant Roman general who fought in many a successful campaign before dying of a mysterious stomach ache after a row with his wife.

It was the task of the best-known soothsayer in all Rome, Bigamus Polygamus, to forecast how long it would take for the emperor's friends to give up the ghost. Caligula selected only a favoured few hundred whom he felt deserved the honour of having him put a dog's leash round their necks and then teach them, after a small libation, to 'Die for their country'. Sometimes Bigamus Polygamus's establishment can't cope with the demand and he subcontracts the job out to a few trusted seers. This is obviously one of those times.

It is an onerous task for an experienced soothsayer as it involves sacrificing to the God of upset stomachs, scattering the bones of a previous victim of a poison practitioner – or, as they now like to call themselves, physicians – and sometimes having to read the signs and portents of the heavens above.

If all this fails, I usually throw a house rat in the barrel and, if it has stopped swimming by the time it takes to boil a bowl of soup, then it is unfit enough to pass for human consumption. As this is a bit of a rush job, I decide to run with the rat-in-the-barrel test rather than disturb the God of upset stomachs and all the rest of that palaver. I call out for my slave, the Nubian Oderous Flatulensius. My friend Ali Minium, an Arab who had a second-hand slave-trading concession, brought him to Rome. Ali informed me his tribal name was Mipapsrtender. But, as this had connotations in our language, I decided to spare his blushes by giving him a proper Roman name. I also promised him his freedom if he could wangle it to get Ephesa to leave me. So far, he is, unfortunately for both of us, still in my service.

'Oderous,' I call out, 'I need a rat. It's for poisoning so don't bring me a pet one. One of the ones that play down by the compost heap will do.' From somewhere within the confines of the house, Oderous breaks wind once to signify that he is on his way to get me an appropriate rat. He is, unfortunately, dumb so I allow him to communicate by breaking wind – once for yes and twice for no. Fortunately, he is blessed with a digestive system that can handle just about any comestible challenge. This, however, has the unfortunate side effect of an olfactory essence emanating from his rear that leaves one's eyes stinging. On the upside, the noise that accompanies his emanations is loud enough to be heard anywhere in the household. Indeed, when he and Ephesa are discussing the daily chores, it has been likened, by more than one passer-by, to thunder shouting at an erupting volcano. It is, for obvious reasons, always a good idea to frame any question so that Oderous can reply in the affirmative.

It is while I am waiting in the courtyard for Oderous to dig up a suitable rat that I receive a visit from Tedium Valium, one of the most boring senators in all Rome. Tedium is one of those annoying men who think that, just because they've reached debilitating senility, this somehow has given them great wisdom and insight. To be fair to him, as a bore, he is quite exceptional. He has a talent that is given us by the Gods and can't really be taught – the talent being that his ability to bore knows no confines. He can, with no effort, bore on any subject that one comes up with. Most politicians have it to some degree but Tedium takes it on to another plane altogether.

He also excels at telling you things that are patently obvious. 'Ah, Julius Jollius, I see you are alone,' he states, proving my point straight away. 'A full barrel of red wine, eh?' he continues irritatingly. 'Might I have a glass? It is hot today, isn't it? Cooler in the shade, though, I've noticed,' he continues relentlessly, while handing me a glass that, believe it or not, he carries around with him.

'My dear Tedium, nothing would give me greater pleasure than to give you a glass of this wine,' I reply truthfully. 'However, it is from the emperor's own cellar and is here for testing – if you get my meaning?' I say, hinting heavily.

The doddering old dolt, of course, gets the wrong end of the stick altogether. 'You think he might notice that a glass had been taken? What an interesting observation! One, however, that may not stand up to the harsh reality of the honed intellect of a senior member of the Roman Senate, such as myself.'

He grates on, 'If you will indulge me for a moment, I will reveal the flaw in your logic, my dear Jollius. For the sake of argument, let us empty the barrel, one glass at a time, into another . . .' he pauses to emphasise this next bit, 'this time EMPTY barrel and, by the way, I will be happy to oversee the experiment for you for a fraction of my usual fee,' he intones. 'I think you will find that the overall effect of one glass less would be impossible to detect. I submit, therefore, that, even with the divine gifts bestowed on our illustrious emperor, Gaius Caligula, he would not be able to detect that one glass is missing from the barrel.' His boring monotone continues, 'Why don't you start emptying the full barrel into the empty one now and we can begin the experiment right away.'

I have had enough. 'No need, Tedium Valium,' I say with a nod of my head that signifies deep respect. 'The paucity of your patrician logic, as always, shines through with a luminosity that invades us mere proletarians with awe,' I waffle on.

He waves a hand in the acknowledgement that he finds no trouble accepting the logic of this statement. 'Please accept a glass of the emperor's wine which, as you have so ably demonstrated, he will never miss.' As I hand him the lethal libation, I muse that one more ancient senator stuffed with his own self-importance would probably never be missed either.

As Tedium sips at his wine, Oderous appears carrying a small sack containing the rat I had called for, which, judging by the way it was writhing around, knew it was ripe for a lethal wine-tasting session. 'It's all right, Oderous, I don't think I'll need the rat after all. Would you take it back to the compost heap?' With a nod of his head and a blast from his bum he signals OK and turns back, taking with him the luckiest rat in Rome.

'Talking of the divine Caligula, you know, of course, that he has declared himself a God?' he witters on, again imparting information that was at least a year old.

As I listen to him, I muse that the rat in the compost heap had more sense than to talk itself into an impromptu duel with mortality. 'How's the wine?' I ask.

'A bit on the sour side,' he complains.

'That'll be the hemlock,' I muse, inwardly, before deciding that, tempting as it was, I really cannot be responsible for the death of even this boring old fart. 'Let me get rid of it and I'll give you some decent stuff of my own,' I say, reaching out for his glass which, I notice, is only missing a few drops. 'I had a look at the stars last night on your behalf, Tedium, and I foresaw that you may have a bit of an upset tum-tum today. So I should stock up on something that will induce retching to expel whatever may be the cause,' I inform him while crossing to the doorway of the house and hailing Oderous. 'Bring back the rat and fetch a jug of wine while you're at it.' A WHOOOMF, from somewhere up the stairs, informs me that Oderous is back on the case.

'As I was saying,' Tedium carries on, 'our divine emperor has declared himself a God. I believe he has chosen the form of Almighty Jove as the entity he has now metamorphosed into. Or, indeed, it may have been that Jove chose the emperor. You know that's a question that has not been raised in the senate.'

146

The pupils of his eyes drift up until they disappear behind his eyelids. While this is happening, he continues to have verbal intercourse with himself. 'How interesting, eh, Jollius? Would a God choose an emperor or would it be more fitting for an emperor to choose a God. And, indeed, further to that hypothesis, should an emperor choose a lesser God and work his way up the divinities or, and here's another interesting point, would choosing a lesser God be construed as an insult by the greater Gods? Or could an emperor take the form of a Goddess? NOW, there's another fascinating hypothesis.'

I'm thinking of another hypothesis entirely. Should I sit here listening to more of this or should I crawl into a hot bath and slit my wrists? A loud splash interrupts my deliberations as Oderous throws the rat into the wine. How quickly our fortunes change, I muse. Just a moment ago, the fates of Tedium Valium and Rattus Verminius were reversed, thanks to the God Julius Jollius.

'What was that noise?' Tedium voices as his eyes come back down from examining the inside of his head.

'What noise was that?' I voice back.

'My dear Jollius, didn't you hear it? It was a splash of some kind.'

'Where did it come from?'

'I'm not sure – I was examining the inside of my head at the time.'

'Can you really do that? Amazing. How on earth do you manage to do something as clever as that? Can all of our illustrious senators do such a thing?' I reply, feigning interest.

'Indeed, no – there's only myself as far as I am aware. Look, I'll show you me doing it, if you like?' his voice quivers with the excitement of the moment as he forces his pupils up the inside of his eyelids. 'I'm doing it now. Notice how my pupils disappear from my eyes entirely and all you can see is the whites of my eyes.' They have, indeed, disappeared. I presume he has never been told that the whites were now a mixture of red and liverish yellow. I'm not sure whether this is due to his advanced age, the early signs of jaundice or the emperor's wine starting to take effect.

'I can still see some of the pupils, Tedium,' I lie, mischievously. This seems to act like some form of challenge and I notice he is starting to groan slightly with the pain as he strains to shove the pupils higher up into the back of his head. However, it does have the advantage of taking his mind off the sound of a half-pissed rat rapidly approaching total inebriation.

'Can you still see a bit of pupil, Jollius?' Tedium groans. The knuckles on his hands are now an intriguing off-white colour as they blanch with the effort of gripping the arms of his chair.

'Yes but surely you can't make them disappear altogether. That would be too amazing for words.' I hear the rat burp loudly as Tedium redoubles his efforts. Little grunts of pain intermingle with gasps as he pursues this act of inanity. 'That is extraordinary. They are going further back and have now ALMOST disappeared altogether,' I carry on, murmuring to myself as though I'm not speaking to him but rather thinking aloud. 'I suppose as you get older and more – what's the word? – unfit? No that's not quite right – infirm? Yes, that's the word. I was just thinking, Tedium Valium, that the older you get then presumably the harder it gets until, one day, you simply won't be able to fully retract them and that will be a signal that your life is – what's the word? – finished.'

I notice him starting to shake all over, quite uncontrollably, as Oderous removes the rat from the barrel and gives me the thumbs up, accompanied by a bellowing out from the rear end of his trousers which signals mission accomplished. As Oderous leaves the vicinity, Tedium is breathing heavily with his efforts and happens to suck in a bit too much of Oderous's parting gift to the atmosphere. A dreadful gurgling sound rolls around the back of his throat. I can't help noticing that, as his pupils are falling back into their normal position, they also seem to be trying to escape from the anguish of the inevitable stinging sensation that one of Oderous's emissions can bring about. This gives them a peculiar bulging effect which, I have to say, is not very flattering.

When he eventually starts to recover, Tedium remarks that, as well as the sore eyes and singed nostril hairs, he is beginning to feel a trifle queasy in the bowels. 'Just as you foresaw last night, Jollius,' he remarks with what I take to be a touch of admiration. I nod sagely, cast some bones on the ground, invoke the Gods of his household to intercede on his behalf and sell him a potion that the Gods have approved, telling him to take it four times a day and, if he is not better in three days, to come back and see me. By that time, potion or no potion, his body will have disposed, in the usual way, with the small amount of Caligula's wine that he has swallowed.

Shaking me by the hand, he presses twenty-five silver denarii into my grip which immediately tightens round them. 'You are, indeed, a marvel that I wonder at, Julius Jollius,' he says earnestly.

'I wonder about you too, Tedium Valium,' I reply honestly. When he eventually leaves, I put the lid on the barrel and stamp it with the soothsayer's seal of approval. I call loudly for Oderous to deliver the barrel to the emperor's victuallers and prepare an invoice for Bigamus Polygamus. By the time I have finished these tasks, it is nearly time to open up the shop again – nearly but not quite. I reason that I can still indulge in my favourite hobby of lying on my back with my eyes closed. Ephesa remarked once that the Gods had bestowed on me an immense talent for doing nothing – slowly. I have never forgotten her observation as it is the nearest thing to a compliment that I've ever received from her.

I lie on my back and, with a sigh of deep satisfaction, close my eyes and drift off. As I drift, I can feel myself sink into blissful oblivion, leaving behind all worldly woes and going deep into a land of dreams. I always have the same recurring dream. (I suppose, if it recurs, that'll be why I always have it.) In this dream, I am sent by the Gods to father the entire world and, to achieve this end, I wind up living with the ugliest group of beings you can imagine. The one I am partnered with is a dead ringer for Ephesa and the air is rancid with the smell of breaking wind – actually not too different from my life at present, I suppose.

I am in a time where there are no towns or cities. There is not even any mention of the eternal city, Rome. But it is a lovely dream because there is never anyone wanting me to do something urgently. No despotic emperors poisoning people out of nothing more than a whim, no invoices or taxes, no wondering what clothes to wear and how to pay for them. The Gods never punish you for not sacrificing or failing to worship on a holy day. It's just a life of pure unrelenting bliss – apart from the smell, of course. I am not sure if I have been sleeping or merely daydreaming and nor do I know how long I had been floating along in this reverie when I feel the earth shake with the sound of Ephesa in full cry. 'Jollius, wake up! Wake up! Glorious news! The emperor wants you to attend him.' I'm sure I haven't heard her right. As my eyes prise themselves open, Ephesa enters the room, closely followed by Oderous. I give my head a shake to disperse any lingering thoughts about my recurring dream and, for confirmation, ask, 'Did you say the emperor wants me to attend him?'

'Yes! Get up, you lump! Don't just lie there asking stupid questions. There's an official litter waiting outside for you.'

'For me? Why would the emperor want me to attend him?' I ask.

'How do I know?' is Ephesa's unhelpful and hurried response, as she lifts me bodily from my reclining position. 'Just don't make a complete twat of yourself and try to remember everything so you can tell me all about it when you get back, so I can tell the next meeting of the Houses, Mouses, Louses and Spouses Society all about it.' She is stripping me of my working clothes as she speaks and fitting me into my best toga. 'Try and get his autograph and don't eat until after you meet the emperor in case you spill anything on your toga. I am going to ask questions when you return. So, as I said, remember everything that happens.' She twitters on, putting my best wig on top of the sparse greying dome that used to boast a full head of hair.

'Shouldn't that go on MY head?' I question, tentatively.

'Of course,' is her testy reply as she removes the wig from her head. 'You see what you're making me do with your dithering. Put it on yourself if you can manage. Oderous? Is the litter still waiting or has it left?'

As he peers out of the window to check, Oderous's anus barks once in response to the first question and twice in response to the second. My wig curls up at the edges and flies off my head in response to Oderous's anus. Fanning the air, Ephesa ushers us out of the courtyard and round to where the imperial litter does, indeed, await.

Oderous sticks my wig back on my head as Ephesa lifts me on to the imperial litter. No sooner has my bum sunk into the cushions that are carefully placed and we are off. The litter is borne by six slaves who are obviously extremely experienced. As we speed on our way to the Imperial Palace, the litter doesn't bob up and down as if one were on the high seas in a force ten gale, which is the usual experience with public litters – an experience that can leave you (well, me, anyway) with a distinct feeling of seasickness. I'm glad of their expertise as it means I do not spew over my good toga. It also means I can concentrate my mind and try to reason out why I'm being summoned to the presence of the emperor Gaius Caligula.

I have, of course, never been in his presence before and,

knowing his reputation for having people butchered on a whim, I was content to live out my days without the experience. I can only think that he needs a soothsayer and something has happened to Bigamus Polygamus. This, indeed, proves to be the case as, on entering the grounds of the palace, I see Bigamus. Well, actually, what I see is his head. The rest of him has been buried so that just his head and his hands are sticking out from the ground.

As we pass, he gives me a smile, waves one of his hands and shouts out, 'He's in a bit of a mood.'

I smile back and, I admit with not a great deal of originality, can only think to say, 'You're looking well.'

'Thanks,' he responds as we speed past. Then, as if in after-thought, 'Did you get the barrel of poisoned wine I sent round?' I give him the thumbs up. 'Oh good,' he says with a twinkle in his eyes. 'Someone's in trouble, eh? I wouldn't like to be in their shoes. As the poet says, "There's always someone worse off than yourself", eh, Julius? Good to see you again. Enjoy the rest of your day.'

As we speed on, I shout back to him, 'You too!' Just before we round a corner, I see a vulture perch on top of his head which, with my training in foretelling the future, gives me a clue that Bigamus Polygamus might soon be Rigorus Mortus. As panic courses through my body and takes refuge in my bowels, I begin to realise that Ephesa's fear that I might soil my toga with food is not perhaps the worst scenario. When finally we come to a halt, it is at the bottom of a huge cream and black marble stairway. I'm escorted up to a great hallway by four members of the palace guard and, after walking for about a quarter of a mile, I'm brought to a halt again, this time outside an enormous ornate silver and gold door encrusted with the finest Egyptian lapis lazuli.

One of the guards raps three times on the door with the aid of a solid gold knocker representing Zeus. The door finally swings open to reveal a sight that will live with me forever. Never, in my wildest dreams, could I have imagined such opulence. It seems as if the treasures of the entire world have been plundered and placed for the sole purpose of adorning this infinite space. The ceilings (there are three) drip with gold and precious metals that I cannot even give a name to. Paintings of exquisite colours, featuring the pantheon of Gods in their finest attire, almost crush you with the power of their actuality.

As I stand there gawping, I become aware of music being played. A figure descends slowly from the ceiling. Golden wires, as thin as gossamer, were barely discernible behind two huge silver wings attached to its back. It is human in form, covered entirely in gold leaf and playing a lyre. A choir is singing along:

> There was once a young Grecian called Oedipus
> Who was told by his mummy to feed his puss.
> He said, 'After I do,
> Can I go to the loo?'
> Said his Mummy, 'Does Oedipus need a piss?'

Something deep inside tells me to applaud this drivel. Also, having heard tales of the emperor's reputation for dressing up in, shall we say, non-regulation Roman dress, I have a fair idea of who the figure is. Dropping to my hands and knees, I prostrate myself and cry out, in what I hope is my best devotional wail, 'Hail! Hail! Mighty Caesar! Your presence is that of a God come to earth. Accept my supplication and my adoration as but tiny tokens of my undying devotion to your magnificence.' My heart freezes as I hear nothing from him – or even it? – in response. I do not dare look up from my prostration as to have done so could easily result in my joining Bigamus as a novelty vulture perch. I fear the worst when I hear noises of annoyance coming from above me.

'Thith ith infuriating, tho it ith. Hey, you! Whatever your

name ith,' his voice is tinged with more than a touch of petulance, 'if it'th not too much trouble,' the petulance is now heavily laced with sarcasm, 'would you mind getting up and helping me out of thith?' Slowly I look up and see that the emperor is trying to extricate himself from the gold wires that have been used to lower him from above. I arise and, not without trepidation, approach him. He is signalling to someone high above, hidden in the morass of gold, silver and a hundred odd other precious metals that festoon the roof. 'Thlacken off, will you?' he shouts upwards, tugging at the wires. Then, lowering his head, on which there is a curly blonde wig that has been knocked slightly askew from his battle with the suspension wires, his gaze settles on me.

'Are you deaf or thomething? Unhook me at the back here,' he indicates, impatiently pointing to behind his neck with his thumb. 'There ith thomething thticking right into me. It'th giving me gyp, tho it ith.' Never being one who could not respond to a life-threatening moment, I quickly skip round the back of him and see that the wires have got caught up in the wings and caused a tangle. It is the work of a moment to free them. Once I have done so, I step back and assume the position on the floor.

'Oh that'th a relief, tho it ith,' he sighs, before barking further instructions up at the wire-pullers. 'You are a dithgrathe to your profethion. Form a thircle and flog each other merthilethly then report back here thith evening for rehearthalth. OK?' A chorus of disgruntled murmurs descends from above, grudgingly signifying their assent to his orders. 'Fly the thuthpenderth out ath well.' The fact that he is stamping his feet signals his impatience is building. Peeking up from my prone position on the floor, I can see the gold wires disappearing into the tangle of precious metals adorning the ceiling. I also catch a fleeting glimpse, as the wires vanish, of a panel sliding back into position. This is, no doubt, where the emperor had started his descent from heaven. A sound of exasperation passes over my head. However, I can see that he has at least stopped stamping his feet.

'Tho! Who are you then? And get up.'

I rise to my feet and speak, still keeping my head bowed in reverence, 'I am Julius Jollius, a humble soothsayer, whose only joy in life is in serving his emperor, the God Gaius Caligula. You sent for me, Your Highness, and I am here to carry out whatever you order,' I babble on uncontrollably in my utter panic not to be executed. 'Your Majesty's whim is my command. I only hope that it is in my power to carry out the whim for him, whatever the whim is.'

I can hear what I take to be loud laughter explode from him. 'Oh, no! You've got the wrong end of the thtick altogether,' he peels, through a fit of coughing brought about from his cackling. 'I'm not Hith Majethty. But bleth you for thaying it. It'th very thweet of you to think of me in thothe termth. And, trutht me, I won't thay a word to him about your little mikth up. Or he might jutht take the huff with you and thart calling you nameth.'

I smile and reply, 'I don't mind that – sticks and stones may break my bones but names will never hurt me.'

He smiles back and says, 'How about innothent victim, headleth corpthe or thcabbard.'

'Why would he call me a scabbard?' I question.

'A thcabbard ith thomething you thtick thwordth into,' he explains. I take his point.

'May I ask, then, Excellency, in whose wondrous presence do I find myself? I can only surmise that, apart from his magnitude the emperor, you are as close to a living God in his heaven as I will ever see.' I lick his golden boots, which are encrusted with diamonds, just to emphasise that I am on his side.

He is almost purring with pleasure as he says, 'I can't quite put my finger on it but there ith thomething about you that appealth to me. You theem to be very genuine in your fawning.

A lot of the palathe thtaff are exthethive in their flattery. But, refrethyingly, you jutht thay it like it ith. And I like that in a groveller,' he says as I continue with the licking – although I have been forced to move up to the backs of his hand as the jewels in his boots were rubbing at my tongue. 'To anther your quethtion of my identity. I am the emperor'th head of thtaff and thith, thuch ath it ith, ith my offith.'

I prostrate myself again. I have only heard rumours of this man but they are enough to make my blood coagulate. His excesses are legendary – some say even more so than the emperor himself. When I eventually get my voice back, I do not so much speak as pray. 'Does your enormity mean that I am actually in the presence of the All Powerful but Still Magnanimous and Immensely Loved Derriuth Irvinuth?'

His face beams as he replies, 'Yeth, you are'th.' His hand pats the top of my head and then signals me to rise. As I do, I keep my arms outstretched and bob up and down in front of him in what is called, in the Middle East, a salaam. 'Oh, yeth! I love it. You didn't open a vein at the thrill of meeting me but are merely content to thalaam inthethantly. That ith really thtraight from the heart thtuff, that.' I continue salaaming as it seems to have struck a chord. He watches me for a while and then taps me on the head. 'That'th enough. You can thtop now. You're thtarting to make me theathick, watching you. I am thorry about the meth of thith plathe. It'th a tip, I know, but I'm having it done up thoon. I like to ring the changeth at leatht wunth a month. However,' he whispers conspiratorially, 'to make up for the thqualor I am having to endure, the emperor ith making me into the nektht betht thing to a God.'

He pauses for effect before the words rush out from him. 'He ith going to make me a Lord on High. Ithn't that too ekthiting for wordth? I'll be The Lord High Derriuth Irvinuth. I won't ever have to thcrimp and thcrape again.' He spins round and round as he claps his hands together with excitement. Then he stops and says to me, icily, 'You could join in if you felt it appropriate?'

I need no more encouraging. 'I'd love to, my Lord. Would it be too offensive to your Imperial Mint if I whooped with joy at the same time?'

His face shines with delight again, 'Oh, I love the way you think. Let'th both whoop together.' We continue with the whooping and clapping hands as we spin round and round until, mercifully, Derriuth starts to get dizzy and falls into a heap on the leopard skin rugs which are strewn across the inlaid marble floor. He rolls around for a while until he, at last, comes to a halt. Resting his head on an ocelot cushion that has been stuffed with pink-coloured ostrich feathers, he toys with a fist-sized diamond that had been used to plug a mouse hole in the mahogany skirting that surrounds the perfumed cedar wood frieze depicting the victory parade when Gaius Marcius Coriolanus defeated the Corleone family. The most significant feature of the frieze being the moment he wakened up in the middle of the night with a horse's head jammed up his rectum. When asked if he was all right, legend has it he said, 'Nay, I feel a little hoarse.'

Derriuth gazes round the massive space and sighs, 'It'th no uthe. I thyall have to thtart again. It all lookth tho tacky. Fortunately, we can tax the thitithens until they bleed by telling them it'th for pothterity and how it will go down in hithtory and be an educathion for their grandchildren and all that thyit. Oh! I nearly forgot. You're here at the beheth of our divine Caligula. I thupothe I'd better take you to thee him, eh?'

I bend in supplication again and ask if he has any idea why the emperor Caligula wants to see me. He stops grimacing at the room decorations for a moment to say that he hasn't a clue. It could be anything from wanting to promote me to Consul to using me as a meat tenderiser. He also tells me that, when Caligula was a lad, being the son of Germanicus, the famous

Roman general, he had originally been called Little Boots by the soldiers, because he wore little boots (caliga). Later, when he went to Britain, he was called Furry Boots by the inhabitants of somewhere called Aberdeen because the locals asked, 'Furryboots is he?' He warns me never to call the emperor that and also to make sure that I flatter him incessantly. 'He'th not nearly ath rooted in reality ath I am,' Derriuth explains.

'When shall I meet the wonder of the age that is our emperor, Lord Derriuth? I only ask because he sent for me over an hour ago and I would rather cut my right arm off than keep him waiting.'

Derriuth tut-tuts, 'Big mithtake. Never, I repeat never, offer to mutilate yourthelf or commit thuithide in order to pleathe him. Because that'th exthactly what you'll wind up doing. It will altho mark you out ath a total tothpot amongtht the thtaff. The correct palathe etiquette ith to offer to cut thomebody you don't like'th arm off. That, you thee, keepth you at the correct level of total thubmithion and altho total thafety.' He smiles indulgently. 'Don't worry about being late. He athked me to vet you before you had an audienthe – jutht in cathe you needed to be ekthecuted before he thaw you. I know it thounds complicated but it thaveth time in the long run.'

My legs start to shake and my tongue dries out while sweat pours from my greying fear-drenched face. He gazes at me. 'That'th another thing – you're not thyowing enough fear.' He places a hand to his nose and taps it quizzically. 'Here'th a wee tip. Do you think you could vithibly thyake uncontrollably?' I have no difficulty with this and straight away convert his tip into actuality. His head nods in approval. 'Much better. Latht wee tip – when you meet him, whatever you do jutht don't be yourthelf and you'll be fine.' He laughs. 'Relakth – he'th not a monthter. Well, he ith but you know what I mean. OK? Then follow me.'

As I trail trepidatiously behind Derriuth, I wonder if I will ever leave this house of horror. I have always imagined that it would be wondrous to live surrounded by such luxury. Now I am beginning to appreciate my own lifestyle – such as it is – and, at this moment, I would gladly swap a fistful of palace jewels for a bawling-out by Ephesa. Even being locked in a small room with Oderous Flatulensius on a quiz night seemed a preferable option.

As we hurry along what seems to be a myriad of immense corridors, various fear-filled countenances pass hurriedly by, only stopping to prostrate themselves in front of Derriuth. Even in the unreality of the palace, he stands out – well, he would, being completely naked, covered in gold leaf and wearing not only silver earrings but silver bird's wings as well. Bits of gold drop from his body as we hurry along and I notice that there are cleaners at hand to sweep them up immediately. Now, there's a good job. Finally, we come to the most gigantic pair of doors I have ever seen. Before this day, I could not even have imagined that, in all the world, there would be a structure large enough to need such barriers. I'm filled with a fearful curiosity.

At the side of these two enormities are two much smaller doors – one on each side. Derriuth nods, 'He'th inthide through thothe big doorth. I jutht hope he'th not in one of hith moodth.' For the first time, I see fear in his face. Except for the gold leaf, it looks just like the fear that is on mine. Again my bowels show singular concentration by informing me that they need emptying. 'I'm afraid I need a number two, Your Eminence,' I explain through gritted teeth.

He replies, through gritted teeth, that he is in the same boat. 'Your Eminenth needth to become Your Emptineth ath well. It happenth every time, that'th why we built thothe looth at each thide.' I notice that both the smaller doors have little figures painted on them. One is a man crapping himself with fear and the other is a woman doing the same. Above the man, it says 'Fodder' and, above the woman, it says 'Fodderess'.

When we have both relieved ourselves of at least the symptoms, if not the feelings, of terror we stand once more, apprehensively. Derrius turns and asks me if I'm ready.

'I suppose so,' I reply.

'Remember to fawn ath you have never fawned before,' are his last words as he pulls at a fifty-foot silk bell rope. Instead of a bell pealing out, music fills the senses from every angle of the palace. As the doors swing open, it is as if the entire palace has become a sounding horn to usher in whoever dared pull on the bell rope. What meets my eyes stuns my senses. As the doors close behind us, the music fades gently and I am left standing there, mouth agape at the scene. It is as if I have been transported to the home of the Gods. Stretching out before me, at eye level, is what would appear to be the summit of Mount Olympus. Olympus – where the Gods of Greece and, indeed, the Gods of Rome too, it is rumoured, spend their time quarrelling and plotting with each other, as well as causing joy and heartache for we poor mortals who dwell beneath their mighty feet. Little white fluffs of cloud play in between the hillocks of the mountain which is covered with exotic flora and fauna – most of them new to my eyes.

Fruit trees are dripping with dates and pears. Grapevines, apples, oranges, passion fruits and hundreds of succulents delight the eye. In a river that flows between a group of trees and the swell of an embankment, fish rise lazily to pluck brightly coloured insects from the air and then settle, with a gentle plop, back into their liquid home. Birds of paradise mingle with ostriches and peacocks whose plumage seems to be adorned with hitherto undiscovered jewels and gemstones.

'He'th having the whole plathe done over next week ath well. It needth frethyening up. I'll thee if I can contact him.' Deriuth takes up a large horn, made from what looks like some extremely big snail shell, and blows into it. Almost at once, a centaur (a creature that is half man and half horse) gallops up to our side. 'Ith Hith Totality in the vithinity?' The human part, being the front of the centaur, nods its head up and down and whinnies as it rears up, its forelegs pawing at the air. A voice from inside it says in muffled tones, 'I told you not to do that. Your behind keeps banging up against my nose.' It doesn't take a genius to come to the conclusion that all may not be as it seems to be from now on. The front of the centaur is obviously miffed at his counterpart's unprofessional conduct and, to teach him a lesson, he says, 'Sure, jump on my back the both of you and I'll take you to him.'

'You must be joking,' says his rear end.

'No! I can athure you he ith not,' lisped you-know-who.

'Oh, shit!' exclaims the rear end, not inappropriately. 'Sorry, Your Lordship. I didn't know it was you. Please avail yourselves of my unworthy back for a hurl anytime you like.' As we ride towards the emperor, I see various stalls advertising stewed ambrosia, boiled ambrosia, braised ambrosia or the all-day breakfast special – fried egg and ambrosia, with grilled tomatoes, washed down with a jug of nectar – all for a hundred and fifty sestertii, which is not bad value, considering the surroundings.

We come to the top of a hill and get off when the man in the back of the centaur skin collapses with severe spinal damage. About fifty yards away, in a valley of unspeakable beauty, I see a temple. It shines with a lucid radiance that appears to emanate from its very essence. Such is its brilliance that a lake of azure blue seems to be suspended in the air. Leading from this symphony of peace is a pathway strewn with sweet-smelling herbs and rose petals.

It leads to an ornate waterfall where iridescent blue-green water gurgles through the openings of sculptured marble nymphs and fawns, there to join with the lake in a tinkling melody that could have been composed by the Gods themselves. Surrounding this wonder is a hillside constructed from gold inlaid with rare blue marble from the north of Italy. Agate, rubies, opals, pearls and other precious stones from around the world have been used to depict scenes of Diana the Huntress, fleet-footed Mercury, Hercules and Juno – in fact, all the Gods are represented in a depiction that demonstrates to the onlooker that these are the masters of the Earth and that the Sun, the Moon and the heavens are their rightful domicile.

At the heart of all this splendour is an altar a hundred feet long and twenty feet high. It seems to be carved from a single block of purest Parian marble and, on the altar sitting on a massive throne of black onyx outlined with jade and inlaid with turquoise, sits Zeus himself. 'Oh, good, he'th in,' says Derriuth in what I think is a pretty anticlimactic way. 'Fingerth crothed and here we go. Don't forget to thyake uncontrollably.' If ever there was an unnecessary instruction, that is it.

Zeus or, more accurately, Caligula surveys us as we proceed, shaking uncontrollably, to crawl along the ground to where he is sitting. I manage to get a quick glance up at him, from my position of movable prostration, and what I see is very impressive. His hair is a silver mane containing a torrent of waves and curls that cascade round his face, mirroring the waterfall that frames the altar. His countenance is bright of eye and noble and dignified but maybe with just a touch too much lipstick.

It is perched on a quite magnificent physique. Broad, square and powerful shoulders lead to muscular arms outlined by a thick vein that emphasises the bulge of his biceps. Thick gold armlets are clasping at his forearms and wrists. His chest swells with latent power and a single bead of sweat is trickling down to a stomach crammed with knotted muscles that wrestle with each other for prominence. His legs are truly stunning – like tree trunks lined with raw sinews. One arm rests on a mighty thigh while the other holds a golden spear, the bottom end of which is planted firmly on the ground while the sharp point glistens as it reaches upwards to the heavens.

I take all this in with one hasty glance as we both crawl

towards him. His voice rings out, 'Derriuth Irvinuth, who is this that approaches with such deference to the God of all Gods?'

Derriuth whispers, out of the side of his mouth, 'More fear – thyake more or you're hyena meat.' I shake as I have never shaken in my life. Two teeth fall out and my wig flies off and is wafted out of sight by the air flowing from my body's exertions.

'OK, that's enough. I, Zeus, have decided that you will live for at least the next five minutes. Such is the magnanimity of my mercy. Do not mistake it for weakness. Who is this parasitical worm that you have brought into my presence, Derriuth?'

'May I have your permithion to thtop thyaking with un- controllable fear, Your Enormity?' Derriuth quivers. Caligula nods in a gesture that is barely discernible. 'Thith ith Juliuth Jolliuth, the unworthy thooththayer you requethted me to bring to Your Enormity'th illuthtriouth prethenth.'

Caligula's voice again rings out but, this time, it has lost the ring of majesty. 'Oh, thank God you're here!' There is a slight pause before the air is again regaled with majesty as he says, 'I mean, of course, thank me that you are here. As a reward, I will grant you an extension of another five minutes during which I shall not think about killing you. You may speak in my presence in order to thank me profoundly.'

I was never one to look a gift horse in the mouth so I seize my moment. Still prostrate, I begin banging my head on the ground while simultaneously punching myself. 'Divinity,' I mouth whilst raining blows on myself, 'my unworthy life is only a testament to Your Immensity's generosity.' I somehow manage to kick myself as well, which is not easy if you're in the prostrate position. 'My whole being will only be considered worthy of a single breath if I can somehow make Your Magnifi- cence happy for what we mere mortals call a second of time. May I have your permission to continue beating myself senseless in Your Lordship's honour?'

'No! I have something of importance to impart and beating yourself may only become a distraction. I need you to concentrate. You may, as a reward for not displeasing me too much, gaze upon my earthly form. I will now, before your very eyes, perform the miracle of metamorphosis and change from the God Zeus to the God Caligula. Watch and tell all men of the wonder of my powers.'

I look up but remain inert and prostrated. My eyes take in the astounding sight of Caligula's face disappearing from a cut-out hole between Zeus's hair and the top of his neck. What is left is only a painting but a painting of such artistry that, even without a face, it still makes one wonder at its actuality. The real Caligula appears from behind the painting and stands with his arms akimbo. The reality of the new God is patently obvious. His puny arms, legs and torso are offset by the over-made-up face underneath hair that is so thin it is wafting about in the barely discernible breeze. 'Ta-ra,' he sings out.

Derriuth begins to applaud. 'Oh that wath fabulouth. I can never get uthed to it no matter how many timeth I thee it. Wath that not jutht fantathtic, Juliuth Jolliuth?' he urges, elbowing me to shut my open mouth and join him in the congratulations.

'YES! YES!' I proclaim. 'A miracle! Can such wonders exist?' I realise I have forgotten to applaud. 'Mere applause does not do justice to Your Magnitude's magnificence. May I have permission to slap my face in order to try and bring myself out of the spell that I am under in order to worship at the feet of Your Immortality?'

Caligula's face breaks out in a self-congratulatory smirk. 'You may,' he acquiesces as I slap my face repeatedly to make it appear that once is not enough in order to accept the miracle I have just witnessed. Caligula motions us to approach the altar. He is now reclining on an ivory sofa draped with tiger skins. 'I can only remain as the God Caligula for a short time as the other Gods fret when Zeus is away too long, you understand. You may stop slapping yourself for the moment,' he instructs me in a voice that barely rises above a whisper. 'I realise that to be in my presence for too long a time can result in madness for mortals so I will quickly enlighten you as to the purpose of your visit here.'

I have to strain to hear what he is saying because his voice has dropped to a conspiratorial murmur and, for the life of me (literally), I don't want to miss anything he says. 'Have you heard of this new sect that has taken root among the Jews in Jerusalem?' I shake my head. Derriuth shakes his too. 'As a God, of course, I know everything.' I nod. Derriuth nods too. 'My fellow Gods tell me everything. I have been told of this new sect by Jove.'

'Have you, by Jove?' says Derriuth.

'I've just said I have,' says Caligula with a hint of impatience. Derriuth begins to self-mutilate which appeases Caligula enough for him to signal Derriuth to stop it. 'They have, apparently, formed themselves a new religion, fashioned after yet another of their interminable prophets. They really are an exceptionally wearisome people. Their lack of generosity is quite legendary amongst our legions. Apparently, it's said, they are so mean that they only have one God.' He waits for a suitable reaction from us.

We immediately set about splitting our sides laughing. He signals we can stop and I say cajolingly, 'But, Divinity, you are the only God and you are Roman not Jewish.'

'Well, the only one that matters,' he concedes. 'But even I have to have minor Gods to keep me company and stop me wearying with the weight of being so great.' I brush away an imaginary tear from my eye and start to sob softly. 'At last, a mortal with feelings, who understands the burden of being a God. You have touched my heart, Julius Jollius. As a gift for your tenderness of feeling towards me, I decree that I will only

165

execute you in a month that has an "i" in it – unless, of course, I change my mind.' He holds out a foot and I dutifully lick it. 'What was I saying again?'

Derriuth also wipes an imaginary tear from his eye and leaps in, 'You were athking if we had heard of the new thect in Jeruthalem, Majethty.'

Caligula nods in assent. 'You pay attention well, Derriuth. Accept the same reward as the soothsayer – except make it a month with a "b" in it.' Derriuth weeps loudly in gratitude and licks his other foot. 'The new prophet is – or should I say was? – called Joshua bar Joseph. Believe it or not, he was the son of a common carpenter. His followers claim that he can perform miracles and, indeed, some of our legionaries say that they were witness to some such trickery. This all happened during the reign of my Uncle Tiberius so I'm not all that concerned with it.' His voice lowers even more conspiratorially and he leans down towards us. 'However, they say that the night before he was crucified for treason, he drank from a Grail and this Grail assumed magic powers. Now, of course, I have powers beyond tallying but . . .' He leaves the sentence unfinished, hanging in the air.

'Immensity, perhaps a God can never have too many magic powers?' I wheedle cleverly.

His right eyebrow shoots up in an expression of surprise. 'You have pleased me again, Julius. At this rate, I might let you live the year out.'

I salaam in between foot-kissing. 'Your Magnitude's generosity is, indeed, astounding and leaves me, yet again, with a sense of unworthiness.'

He thinks for a moment and then proclaims, 'You're probably right. Cancel that last bequest.'

Derriuth whispers, 'What did I tell you? Don't leave him an opening.'

Caligula sits upright and his voice is no longer confidential.

'What I want you to do, Soothsayer, is find out for me, by studying the signs, where this magic talisman is and bring it to me. I want it to cure my baldness. Of course, as a God, I could cure it myself but . . .' Again he leaves the sentence hanging in the air as he stares at the two of us, waiting for one of us to solve his dilemma.

Derriuth is the first to volunteer. 'It would jutht be too thimple for Your Wonderfulneth to bother with?'

Caligula smiled. 'Correct. As a reward for guessing the right answer to my riddle, you may kiss the sole of my foot as well as the top of it,' he croons. 'However, be careful not to tickle or you could find yourself in a pit full of hungry cobras with a fat juicy rat strapped to your face.' He yawns. 'Cancel that – the audience is at an end. You may both succumb to madness if I tarry longer.' He turns to go and then addresses himself to me. 'I am having some friends for a wine-tasting session this evening. Come along and tell me that you have found the talisman and how you can bring it to me.' With that, he is behind the painting and has become Zeus again. Derriuth and I beat each other mercilessly with some whips that have been provided for that purpose as we crawl backwards from his presence.

On the way back, I ponder, in a panic-stricken way, about my predicament. 'How am I going to find something I've only heard of half an hour ago? And how am I going to report back to him tonight that I've found it? There is no way I can do that. It's impossible. I'll just have to tell him that – he's a reasonable man?'

Derriuth snorts with thinly disguised laughter. 'Of courthe he ith. That'th what Bigamuth Polygamuth thaid – thorry, the late Bigamuth Polygamuth. Ath I thay, I've taken a liking to you tho my advithe ith for you to throw thome boneth about or thtudy an entrail or two, whatever it ith you do and . . .' he winks, 'dithcover that thith Grail ith, thyall we say, in a far off plathe. Perhapth it'th thtill in Jeruthalem? Thuggetht to hith

167

nibth that you will have to leave the country in order to bring it back. That way you get thome breathing thpathe at leatht. It'th either that or you join Bigamuth thtaring up a vulture'th arthe.'

I have to agree with him – especially when, as I'm leaving the palace, I see that all that is left of Bigamus is his wig which is now blowing aimlessly around the courtyard.

As I enter the front door of my house, Ephesa rushes to meet me. 'Did you get the emperor's autograph? What did he want to see you about? Did he contribute to our Houses, Mouses, Louses and Spouses appeal? Well, don't just stand there – say something.' Being a soothsayer, I have foreseen most of these questions and have obtained a signed likeness of the emperor by the process of writing it myself. As I hand her the tablet with the signature, she grasps it from me and reads it out, 'To Ephesa. Best wishes. Yours aye, the God Caligula. XXX.' She's ecstatic. 'What about the appeal did he mention it?'

I explain that, indeed, he did and, furthermore, he wants to make it his primary concern for the next year. To which end he is sending me on a trip to drum up worldwide support and that I have to go back that night to the palace to tie up the details. She, of course, inevitably asks if mention of her was made. To which I inevitably reply that it was and that he never stopped talking about her and her great work as chairwoman of the Houses, Mouses, Louses and Spouses Society.

When she says she can't wait to see him at the palace tonight, I have to do some quick thinking. Almost without a pause, I explain that he wants the whole project kept very hush-hush or his enemies in the senate might refuse to grant him the huge cost involved in supporting the HML and S appeal. 'But I thought he didn't have any enemies. He's reported to have murdered them all?' she quizzes, the usual note of suspicion, which had been strangely absent, creeping back into her psyche.

'Yes! He has, my little force for darkness. That's why he sent me the poisoned wine so I could foretell that its potency is adequate to rid him of the last of the whiners who want to scupper your appeal. That's why secrecy is paramount and, unfortunately, that's why you can't accompany me tonight. But the emperor did say that, once I get back and the appeal is up and running, we will all go up to his place for a celebration.' On hearing this, Ephesa can't wait to get me out the house – she even washes and irons my best toga. In her excitement, she also forgets to give me an ear-bashing for getting it dirty.

I am picked up and dispatched back to the palace by litter and there I'm escorted to an antechamber outside of Derriuth's dressing room. There I am to wait for him to accompany me to the wine tasting. After half an hour or so, I am told he is ready and ushered in to his dressing room. The usual gold drips from the drapes and the entire wall is fitted with silver so polished that you can see your reflection from any angle. The candlelight flickers to darkness. I'm feeling a trifle uneasy when the room bursts into light and Derriuth is revealed. His headdress is that of a golden eagle. The wings drape down the sides of his arms and hands – hands that now have talons at the end of his fingertips. His entire body has been painted with the usual gold leaf except, this time, the detail depicts the feathers of the eagle. His feet are also shaped in the manner of an eagle's and have claws protruding from his toenails.

He shakes his head with dismay as he says, 'Thank the Godth it'th not fanthy dreth tonight or I would have had nothing to wear.' Offering me his arm, he continues, 'Thyall we?' and off we go. On the way, Derriuth informs me the emperor has instructed that the evening is to be informal. 'Wine and nibbles,' is how he puts it. The wine I already know about. The nibbles is a dish known as 'Camel Surprise'. It was introduced to Rome by Cleopatra and consists of a camel stuffed with a cow, stuffed with a pig, stuffed with a peacock. The peacock is stuffed with starlings and the starlings are stuffed with eggs.

I suppose, if you were a camel, you couldn't help but be surprised.

The evening goes well. I tell His Divine Master the God of Everything That It Was Worth Being A God Of that I have studied the portents and have seen a sight that I have never seen before in my life – three blind mice chasing a farmer's wife. Soon after, I also see a young girl taking lunch, sitting on a tuffet, when a spider drops on her bowl of whey and frightens the girl so much she runs off screaming. Lastly, I see, in the embers of my soothsayer's fire, that there is, indeed, such a vessel or Grail. I tell him that it has been hidden by another God who is insanely jealous of Caligula's greatness.

'Neptune, my old enemy. Of course! It's him isn't it?' he screams. 'He's never forgiven me for plundering his treasures. I'll teach him to cross swords with Zeus. I'll outwit him yet again. What is he? Nothing but the God of Dampness – that's all.' He dissolves with laughter at this example of his divine wit. The emperor's pals, still quaffing his wine, join in, laugh, applaud and then drop dead. 'My wit is so wondrous that they've all died laughing,' he observes, wrongly, before turning on me. 'Where is this magical Grail? Find it and bring it to me. If you do and it cures my baldness, I-I-I'll make you a God too.'

I foresee it is time to get going so I tell him that the Grail in question is in Judea and I will go there, as a servant of his divine will, find it and bring it back. While he is cackling insanely and encouraging Neptune to sit on his middle finger, I manage to inveigle the emperor into allowing Oderous to accompany me. A ship is put at my disposal and, with Caligula's warning to watch out for Neptune ringing in my ears, I set sail for Judea. Actually, the crew of the ship set sail – I settle down for a nice kip.

TRANSCRIPT FROM THE JOLLY TAPES

Major Day's voice whipped across the room. 'Well what do you think? Could this be it?'

'Es fer es Eh'm eware, Jesus was crucifehd long before Celiguleh got to this stage in his rule ehs emperor,' mused Mee. 'So how is Jolly – or should Eh say Julius? – going to get hold of the Grail?'

'That thought crossed my mind too,' said the Major.

"Ehnd also,' continued Mee, 'weh should he bother? If he goes beck, he hes to take up with Ephesa ehnd face the mehd Celiguleh – both are options which he seems singularly disinclehned to take up. Ehnd, frenkly, Eh don't blame him.'

The Major's tone of voice was not optimistic when he said, 'So, should we bring him round, try to get him more accurately placed and have another stab at it? Miss Wonterland what do you think?'

Has Kmee Hwy's voice sounded puzzled as he offered the news, 'She's not here.'

'Not here? How do you mean? Where did she go?' said Major Day startled.

'I don't know,' replied Hwy. 'I was concentrating on Jolly.'

The others agreed that that had been the case with them too. 'There's a note here,' Hwy informed them. Then, picking it up, he read out, 'Have gone down to the chemist to get some corn plasters and a new pumice stone. I'll bring back some bickys for tea as the cheese footballs seem to be finished. Allyson.'

With more than a slight note of annoyance in his voice, the Major announced, 'Gentlemen, it looks as if we shall have to wait until Miss Wonterland comes back as none of us have the expertise to a) bring Jolly round or b) send him back into a trance.'

The others silently concurred before Has Kmee Hwy informed the company, 'He's stretching. Could be he is wakening up.'

The Very Reverend Mee spoke all their thoughts when he asked, 'Yes, but when, he comes round, will he be in eh room with us in the Scottish Heghlends or on eh boat sailing for Judeeheh?'

'Where?' asked Hwy.

'Judea,' answered the Major.

'Thet's what Eh sehd,' said Mee.

END OF TRANSCRIPT

I have a lovely kip and am informed by another passenger that we have made great speed due to the captain feeding Oderous a diet of fruit and vegetables and then pointing his rear end at the sails. The captain offers to buy him from me but then withdraws his offer when the crew unplug their nostrils and, complaining about the stinging in their eyes, threaten to mutiny. Our journey has taken us from Rome, through the Strait of Messina where, skirting the Ionian Sea, we speed past Crete, southern Turkey and join the Sea of Galilee before docking at the tiny wine port of Al Kah Hawliikz which is famous for not exporting the delicious wine that they made.

From there, Oderous and I join a caravan heading for Jerusalem. We arrive in this ancient and holy city of the Jews around nightfall and set about seeking out a resting lodge. Most of the lodges are full as there is a big meeting of the followers of Solomon the builder who call themselves Masons and, unless you know the password, they won't let you rent a room. They seem very friendly otherwise and are continually inquiring after my granny and asking how old she is. They seem very disappointed when I tell them she's dead and, in an effort to cheer me up, tickle the palm of my hand with a finger when we shake hands.

Eventually, we find a place where the proprietor has never heard of my granny and, more importantly, has a room to let. Over a meal of matzo bread and kosher meat, I ask him about Joshua bar Joseph and his followers. He remembers him and how he excited the people and raised their hopes that he was the Messiah. However, it appears he offended the Sanhedrin, who are apparently the legal representatives of the Jews, and they pressed the Roman governor, Pontius Pilate, to have him executed. It seems a bit harsh to me and I make a mental note to keep out of their way.

I slip in a question regarding the Grail to the owner, 'Do you know anything about the Holy Grail that is associated with

Joshua bar Joseph?'

'You refer to the last meal that he had with his followers?' he says, leaning into me and dropping his voice to a whisper. I nod in assent. He nods at me nodding. 'Go to the corner of the Street of a Thousand Foetid Fish. There you will find that which you seek.' As is the normal reaction I have when I am excited, my heart races inside my chest. Oderous responds with his customary reaction. The owner leans heavily on my shoulder and, wiping the tears from his eyes, adds, 'Take him with you. He will blend in nicely.'

I can barely wait to finish my meal such is my agitation. On the one hand, I don't really care much for returning to Rome but, on the other, if I do find this Grail, the emperor's gratitude could perhaps know no bounds. I resolve to visit the Street of a Thousand Foetid Fish tomorrow after we have rested from the day's exertions. I go up a flight of stairs to my room to try and rest. Oderous goes down a flight of stairs to the cesspool to try and mingle. Eventually, we both fall into the arms of the God of sleep.

TRANSCRIPT FROM THE JOLLY TAPES

The entire room was in a heightened state of tension and expectation. Even Miss Wonterland, who had returned with a packet of Iced Gems, was starting to appreciate what was at stake and the momentum that was building was almost touchable.

'It's beginning to look as if we may pull it off after all,' the Major said, trying not to sound too anxious as he paced the room tugging lumps of hair out of his head.

Ewen Mee concurred, 'Eh always sehd theht, if we just kept believing, then, eventuelly, Jolly would come good. He's thet type of chep.'

Has Kmee Hwy responded likewise, 'This could be the biggest breakthrough in Tibetan metaphysics since the prayer wheel!'

Miss Wonterland observed, 'He's starting to twitch at the corners of his mouth. Could be he's going to start speaking again.'

The Major quietened everyone down by saying, softly but pointedly, 'I think we may be about to witness one of the most remarkable events in world history.' He placed his hands in front of him, crossed his fingers and then placed them behind his back. Solemnly, the rest did likewise.

END OF TRANSCRIPT

It is a fine morning. The sky is settled and heralds the promise of a good day to come. After wandering around, my nose signals to me that Oderous and I have, at last, come to the district of the Street of a Thousand Foetid Fish. 'This looks like the place, Oderous,' I venture. Oderous's head nods and his sit-upon assents in its usual fashion but I notice that my eyes don't sting. Taking this as confirmation of our whereabouts, we walk to the corner as instructed by my informant of last night. There we notice an inn with a faded sign above the door.

We enter and find ourselves in a dark but surprisingly clean establishment. There is a long table with a bench at each side obviously for the benefit of diners to sit on. A tall man with a marked stoop enters from somewhere at the back of the establishment. He throws open three wooden windows, allowing light to permeate the room, and he speaks in the harsh guttural dialect of a man born to the city. 'What'll it be, gents?'

I give him my smile that I always imagine says, 'Trust me, I'm a soothsayer'. 'Some wine and also some information.'

He studies me for a while and then rasps, 'The price of the wine is marked on the wall. The cost of any information is negotiable.'

I throw a silver piece on the table, saying, 'I'm looking for the Holy Grail.'

He snatches at the silver piece and stuffs it somewhere deep inside the folds of his garment then sits down beside me. 'You're in it,' is his reply.

I can't grasp his meaning. 'I don't understand.'

He motions me to follow him. When we get outside, he points to the faded sign. 'See.' I follow his eyes upwards till I focus on the sign. I can just make out the writing – 'The Inn of the Holy Creel'. I am, quite frankly, more than a bit puzzled. 'I'm looking for the Holy Grail not Creel. What in the name of the Gods is a Creel anyway and why is it holy?'

He points back up to the sign, his hand outlining a box-like contraption with holes in it. 'A creel is for catching lobsters. The lobster goes in and then gets trapped. The holes are in it to let water flow freely.'

I am furious. 'I'm not paying a silver coin for that,' I tell him. 'You just have,' he tells me back.

'But I wanted information about Joshua bar Joseph and his followers.' He shakes his head. 'The Rabbi who was eating in here before he was taken away and executed?' I continue.

His head again signifies mystification. Then a light shoots into his eyes. 'Oh! You mean the big fisherman's friend – the one who got on the wrong side of the Sanhedrin. That was before my time.' As my face falls in disappointment, he says, 'However, for another silver coin I could tell you the whereabouts of the previous owner. He would be able to tell you everything you want to know.' His hand shoots out from the garment folds.

I can see there is nothing to be done but give him what he wants. His greedy eyes glow as he snatches another silver piece. He beckons us back inside and indicates that we should sit. Two beakers of wine are placed before us. 'The man you want is called Alphaeus son of Josiah. He runs a second-hand shop at the corner of the Street of a Thousand Belligerent Beggars.'

My curiosity is roused. I wonder how he could make a living in amongst so many beggars. 'What does he sell?' I ask.

'I told you – second hands. They cut off a hand to beg during the day but then, at night, when they go out for the evening, they strap a false one on for the sake of appearances. Go to Alphaeus. Tell him that I, Malachi son of Josiah, sent you and that you want to find out about the fisherman's friend.'

I think for a moment before venturing the question, 'You're Malachi son of Josiah?' He nods. 'I thought you said that Alphaeus was the son of Josiah?' His head inclines to the left in a quick dismissive gesture. 'He is. Josiah was a bit of a lad.'

There is nothing further to be gained by more questioning so we finish the wine, get directions from him and proceed to the Street of a Thousand Belligerent Beggars. As we enter the street, I approach a beggar to ask if he knows the exact location of Alphaeus's shop. As I produce a few shekels, he looks up from where he's sitting and shouts, 'Piss off! I don't want your charity – stick your shekels!'

All the way down the street, we are subjected to similar abuse. I see Alphaeus's second-hand shop out of a corner of my eye and we run for it. A tin cup bounces off my head as Oderous and I barge through the entrance. A small man with large whiskers sits at a bench carving a hand from a block of wood. He looks up, takes us both in with a single glance and then goes back to his carving. 'I only supply the hands – I don't cut them off,' he says in the same guttural dialect used by Malachi.

'We are not here to purchase a hand,' I inform him, throwing yet another silver piece on the bench. 'I seek information. Are you Alphaeus son of Josiah?' His glance is guarded. Only the whiskers quivering around his jowls give away the interest he is showing in the silver piece that rests near him.

Placing the wooden hand he is carving over the coin, he looks up. 'Who wants to know?'

I lean against the wall of the shop. 'I have been sent from Rome, on the emperor's instructions, to find a certain object. I have been told by Malachi son of Josiah you may be able to help. You are, I hope, Alphaeus son of Josiah?'

Again, he eyes me slowly and with distrust. 'I am.' He shifts his gaze to Oderous. 'Are you from the emperor too?'

Before I can stop him, Oderous replies in his own inimitable fashion. As the full impact of it hits him, Alphaeus experiences the noviciate's reaction to Oderous's olfactory assault. First, the drying up at the back of the throat as one's breathing ceases, then splits developing in the hair ends. The purple rash breaking

ONE DEITY AT A TIME. . .

out. Then the eyes starting to burn and leap out of their sockets resembling an unwell goldfish, before inevitably the final and terrible stinging takes over, leaving you to tear at your eyes and beg for blessed relief. Over the years, one develops a certain immunity to it but, a bit like sex, you always remember the first time.

He eventually comes to and gasps, 'I have heard rumours of the emperor's cruelty but I had no idea that it went to that extent. Tell me what it is you want to know.'

I decide to strike while the eyes were hot, so to speak, and relate the fable of the Holy Grail and how it has been explained to us. Needing confirmation, I ask, 'What's it all about, Alphaeus?'

Wiping the still-flowing tears from his eyes, he swigs from a jug of wine and then, pocketing the silver piece he begins to tell of the night in question. 'It was the Passover supper and I remember that I'd had a booking from Joshua bar Joseph or, as he was also known, the fisherman's friend. I only knew him as a customer but he was well loved by his friends and many of the population. The beggars all worshipped him. For me, he was a regular who always paid and there was never any drunkenness or rowdyism. That night was different, though. There was an atmosphere among them and I remember thinking one in particular was behaving very peculiarly.'

He rubs at an eye and then continues, 'Of course, later on, we all found out why he was behaving strangely. It turned out that he had taken money to inform the soldiers of the whereabouts of his big friend. With friends like that, who needs enemies, eh? That's all I know of that night but the rest of what happened to him is not exactly a secret. He was, as you probably know, eventually crucified, of course.'

I suck in my breath. What he has told me does not help with the Grail. 'That is, indeed, fascinating. However, what the

179

emperor wants to know is the whereabouts of the Grail that Joshua bar Joseph drank from that night. It has become a bit of an obsession with him and, if you could remember . . . Well, it would save me having to ask my friend to propel any more pungency from . . .'

He leaps in before I can finish, 'Mercy, ask me any question. I will answer it but, please, not that,' he begs as his knees hit the ground in supplication.

'Well, as long as you're sure?' I smile before asking, 'What can you remember about the meal itself?'

He thinks for a while, obviously reaching into the back of his memory. I toss him another silver coin. He snaps his fingers, claps his hands together and then announces that it has all come back. 'The meal was for thirteen. Because most of them were fishermen, they ordered fish. At that time, I also did a special dish that was very popular with clients. It was turnip but, instead of boiling it, I used to get a sharp knife and chip the turnip into thin slices and fry it. I called them chips for short.' He pauses as though waiting for a round of applause.

I, however, want to get on with what happened to the Grail. 'How clever of you,' I remark. 'So they all had fish and chips.'

'Yes, that's what they had. I believe that, now I am no longer there, they don't serve the chipped turnip anymore which is a big mistake as far as . . .'

I cut in to his ramblings, 'Yes! As I said – fascinating. What else did they have apart from fish and chips?'

Again, he thinks deeply. I toss him another silver coin and again he snaps his fingers. 'They did not all have fish and chips,' he declares. 'There had been a run on fish that whole week and we only had enough fish for twelve. Bar Joseph said he would do without and just have some bread and water, which he would change into wine, and maybe a bit of cheese.'

I feel we are getting somewhere now. 'The wine? Can you remember what he drank the wine from?' I question, trying not to show my impatience with his wittering on about fish and chips.

'Yes, indeed I can,' he smiles.

'Well, what was it?' I shout, maybe starting to lose it slightly.

'It was a jug,' he informs me, stiffly.

'Are you sure it wasn't a silver cup or any kind of cup. I was told that he had a Grail – a Holy Grail?'

He looks at me askance. 'You know it's funny – a lot of people have asked me that.' He looks meaningfully at my purse. I look meaningfully at Oderous's backside. He capitulates and says, 'You were in my old place. Did it look to you as if the customers drank out of silver cups? No, it was a jug. They all passed it round and then I threw it away at the end of the night because it had fallen and got cracked during the washing up.'

I am crestfallen. My dreams of being among the high and mighty and possibly even made a God are in tatters along with the sought-after Holy Grail. Alphaeus is still reminiscing. 'However, I hated to see the big chap go without because of the fish situation but then I remembered that we had some poultry left over. I asked him if he'd like that instead. He asked me what it was. I told him it was quail. He said that was fine but he wasn't all that hungry and a half of one would do. I gave the order through to the kitchen for twelve fish and chips and one half portion of quail and chips. I seem to remember that the chef said the quail was not very big and that a half portion would not amount to much. I told bar Joseph that the quail was a bit on the wee side and he would be better off having the whole quail. "I'll do it for the same price as the half," I told him. I think that act of generosity on my part swung it because he agreed to have the whole wee quail. I shouted through to the kitchen that bar Joseph would have "THE WHOLE WEE QUAIL".'

My mind seems numb – as if it has totally seized up. 'Are you all right?' asks Alphaeus. 'You look quite pale.'

I realise I have almost fallen from my seat because of the impact of what I have heard. 'I'm fine. It's just that I was kind of pinning my future on finding the cup that has gained fame all over as the Holy Grail and now I find out there is no such thing. It was just someone mishearing "the whole wee quail" as "the Holy Grail".'

I am very downcast and do not respond right away when he says, 'Maybe I can help you out there, sir.' I look at him, not quite taking in what he is saying. He rises from his knees and walks towards an inconspicuous wooden cupboard. 'I can help you in your quest, sir. I can give you that which the emperor seeks.'

He opens the cupboard and there on a shelf stands a cup. It is a beautifully carved and polished piece of workmanship and is, indeed, a vessel fit for a God to drink from. I stare at it for a moment, not quite taking in what I am seeing. Alphaeus's voice interrupts my thoughts. It is trembling with emotion. 'If bar Joseph was who he said he was, then I would honour him by carving out the finest work I was capable of. There, in front of you, is the result of that endeavour.' Tears are now welling up in his eyes as his head lifts and he stares at the cup. 'It took me six months of sometimes fruitless searching to finally track down the finest mahogany and another year to carve out, from a solid block, that which you see before you.' He sits, staring at his gnarled and hardened hands, and sighs. 'I believe he was a carpenter too.'

My gaze drifts back to the cup. I see that there is an inscription saying 𝕿𝖍𝖊 𝕳𝖔𝖑𝖞 𝕲𝖗𝖆𝖎𝖑 on the bottom of it and underneath that is another inscription that reads 𝕬 𝕻𝖗𝖊𝖘𝖊𝖓𝖙 𝖋𝖗𝖔𝖒 𝕵𝖚𝖉𝖊𝖆. I pat him on the back and ask if he will consider selling me it for ten gold pieces. Rising from his chair, he takes the Grail down and looks at it fondly. 'I knew this day would come.' He kisses it and I hand over the gold coins.

I take it from him and wrap it deep inside my wool garment

for safety. 'I would not like to lose it,' I explain.

'Perhaps you would like a spare in case you do?' he replies, opening up another cupboard crammed with Holy Grails.

After the usual haggling, I buy them all. I decide I will set fire to them but keep the original. After a final threat of sending Oderous back for a visit if he makes any more, Alphaeus agrees to stop production. We dine at the Inn of the Holy Creel, book passage and set sail for Rome late this evening. As our ship leaves the quayside, I hope that I am doing the right thing by going back. I would ask Oderous's advice but my meal is not fully digested and I don't want to risk losing it. The thought of being made a God by Caligula is very tempting. There has never been a God in our family and I can't help but wish my dear departed father was still alive to witness my deification. Of course, I daydream, once I am a God, I could maybe fix that?

We set sail in the early evening. Despite a prevailing head wind, with the help of Oderous's answering in the negative to a succession of questions which were framed towards that end, the subsequent tail wind achieved by pointing his anus at the sails ensures we make good time. The captain is so grateful he gives me an upgrade. The upgrade consists of being given a fishing line to throw over the side of the ship. This means that, if you catch a fish, you don't have to eat the slops that the rest of the passengers are given.

I am sitting next to an Arab merchant. As we sail, I notice that he is catching fish when no one else is. Eventually, I ask him his secret. Turning to me he says, 'Roo raff roo ree ri rurms rorm.' I inform him that I don't speak Arabic. He shakes his head at me and says again, 'Roo raff roo ree ri rurms rorm.' Again I signal that I don't understand him. At that he spits out an ugly brown sludge into the palm of his hand and says, 'You have to keep the worms warm.'

His name is Ali Son of Agun and he is on his way to Rome to buy a wife as he only has seven at the moment. Eventually,

I find out that he is the father of thirty-five children. I ask him how he copes with them all. 'Wisdom,' he says, 'is the key to being a good husband and father. Never, I repeat never, lift your hands to a member of your family – it leaves your groin unprotected,' he explains.

Gradually, we become friends and, throughout the journey, we talk of many things. He tells me he set out to be a philosopher but the pressures of providing for a family forced him towards commerce. However, like me, he still likes to contemplate the enigmas of life and we do wonder together on such mysteries as: If it's true that we are here to help others, what are the others here for?; Why are there no gruntled workers?; Why does a woman say, 'We need to talk.' when she means, 'I need to complain.'?

As we converse late into the night, the wind changes and Oderous's anus is no longer required. Apart from a few singed nostril hairs, his efforts have caused no untoward ill effects. We all settle down to pass the night and drift off into the arms of Morpheus, lord of sleep.

A crash like thunder shakes me out of my dreams and I awake to find that the ship is being tossed around like a piece of driftwood in seas that are decidedly treacherous. My hands grab for something, anything, to hold on to. A scream assails my ears and I turn round to see that our main mast has broken in two and disappeared over the side, carrying the captain and at least three crew members with it.

Water is deluging over the side of our ship and I am swallowing salt water with every buck and dip of the beleaguered vessel. Even in the advanced state of panic that I suddenly find myself in, reason tells me that we are not going to see this night out. A colossal wave smashes against us and our inadequate ship rears up on her bow, trying, with one final gallant gasp, to stay afloat. For a second that seems like an eternity, we seem to be in mid air – safe and away from the raging seas beneath – but then, horror upon horrors, hell beckons and we plummet, with dreadful speed, to the merciless seas that rage below. There is a moment of surreal silence as we plunge deep into the enraged foam that swallows us up like a whale would swallow a tiny bit of plankton and then my head bursts through the watery ceiling above and I know I am facing death.

Despairingly, I look for Oderous, knowing that he will fill his trousers with wind and remain afloat no matter what. But, in the torrential turmoil that envelops me, it is fruitless. Then, as I am about to give up and surrender myself to Neptune's revenge for siding with Caligula, I catch the merest glimpse of my friend Ali Son of Agun. He has grabbed hold of a stray oar and it is keeping him afloat. With all my strength, I shout for him to give assistance, 'ALI, HELP!' but salt water smashes against me, drowning out my cries.

Bizarrely, I can feel the Grail, the cause of my being here, crunch into my chest as I am bent double. Then I am shouting out again, 'ALI SON OF AGUN, HELP!' Once more I am swamped. Again, I cry out, 'ALI SON OF . . . ALI-SON!' and, again, cold stinging water invades my throat. I cry out in one last vain attempt to attract his attention, 'ALISONNNNNN!'

'Eh think he meght be coming round,' a voice was strangely ringing around my brain. It was like a pea bouncing around in an empty tin can. 'Jolly, treh to control yourself, mehn. You'll do someone ehn injury if you keep threshing ehbout like thet.'

I could hear what sounded like a woman reply, 'I'll do you an injury, so I will, if you don't stop shouting at the poor man. You're supposed to be a man of God, so you are. Try to show a bit of love for your fellow man, will you?'

'Eh will not be spoken to lek thet beh eh woman with eh serious foot fetish.'

The woman rejoined with, 'You don't know what you're

talking about, so you don't. A foot fetish is when you love feet. I hate my feet.'

'Not ehs much as Eh do, believe me,' was the man's riposte. Both these people seemed to be very agitated. Whatever they were agitated about was of no concern to me. I was content to lie there floating.

'Can I just say,' a third voice cut in on my repose, 'when Jolly comes round fully, I want to hear no bickering? I realise we are all a bit disappointed that our mission has not been entirely successful but that is in no way due to Jolly who, in my opinion, has displayed a courage and devotion to duty that is exemplary and an example to us all.' There was a smattering of applause from various pairs of hands – one of which I realised was mine.

'Eh don't believe it. He's ectually giving himself eh clep,' said someone who sounded like me – or do I mean Mee? Who's Mee?

The woman answered back with, 'You need to give *yourself* a clap – preferably round the earholes.'

I started to drift out of my musing and feel myself being almost sucked out of the comfort of wherever I was and into the present conflict. A flash of white light invaded the inside of my head and suddenly I remembered everything. I had been sent backwards by hypnotic suggestion on a mission to trace the whereabouts of the Holy Grail. Allyson Wonterland was the one who was being suggestive, Major Day was in charge and Has Kmee Hwy and the Very Reverend Ewen Mee were also involved.

'He's opened his eyes.' I stared up into the kind face of Miss Wonterland. Beside her, but lower down, was a face of a kind that, unfortunately for it, belonged to Mee. Stacked up behind them were the other two.

'Welcome back, Jolly,' said the Major warmly.

'Eh hope you ehr feeling all reht,' said Mee hypocritically.

My mind was full of questions, uppermost being: Did I

succeed in tracing the Holy Grail, thereby ensuring my beloved Church of Scotland's supremacy over other religions?; Was God a proddy?; And would I be rich and famous? The answers to these questions, I subsequently found out, were: No; No; and No. I was disconsolate in the extreme. I was so disappointed that it reminded me of my honeymoon with Ephesia. I hasten to add that Ephesia was also disappointed. We had both been told that it would be the most beautiful night of our lives so we stayed up all night looking out of the window so as not to miss it. It rained.

I was assured that I would be given a copy of the tape recordings. The Major made a heart-warming speech about how true faith did not need the buttress of a mythical magical object and that, even although our mission had not yielded up such an object, we had all been brought together in the service of God and would all go away the better for it. None of us believed him but we all thanked him for saying it.

A smell of rancid tobacco and stale fag ends burning in an ashtray mixed with three-day-old cheap hairspray being used as an underarm deodorant introduced Shug. 'I see Rip Van Winkle's joined the land o' the livin' at last,' he slurped through the saliva that inevitably gathered between his lower teeth and his lower lip. 'He can fairly dae the yoghurt, eh? I've never seen anybody menstruate as much as him.'

'I think you may mean meditate,' the Major informed him through the fog of embarrassment that enveloped the room.

'Aye, well, whatever,' Shug said. The words sloshing around his gums. 'Anyway, it's five o'clock – time for me to lock up – so yous'll aw need tae ejaculate the premises.'

With promises in the premises to keep in touch, we said goodnight and went our separate ways. As we left, Miss Wonterland made the most of giving me – and not Mee – two tickets for her next show at the Pavilion. 'You'll have to bring your lovely wife along,' she said with a smile.

'To do thet, he'll hev to remehrry!' said Mee with a bigger smile.

That I had been away from home and Ephesia all day was hard for me to take in. It was going to be even harder to explain why. It occurred to me that I could remember practically nothing of what had happened so to get home and listen to the tapes that had been made while I was in the power of Miss Wonterland's mesmerism was of paramount importance. For the moment, I just had to curb my inquisitiveness and be patient.

Waiting for the bus to whisk me back towards home and a haranguing, I noticed that I happened to be standing outside a smart little shop. As it costs nothing to window-shop, I availed myself of the cheap option. The window was filled with various pieces of bric-a-brac that my gaze flitted over until it rested on one object. It was a ceramic mug with a partridge depicted on it. For some reason, I was much taken with it and decided to take the bull by the horns and enquire about its price.

The door opened to the sound of a bell tinkling in order to let the owner know there was someone in the shop. A small neat woman, probably in her sixties, appeared from the back and welcomed me in the customary manner. 'We're just about to close. Could you not come back tomorrow?' she asked through lips that were so thin they appeared to be just a line drawn underneath her nose. They also did not appear to move when she spoke. 'Well, I suppose you're in now. What is it that you want? And, before you ask, I have noticed that you are a Church of Scotland minister. It's only right and proper you should know that I am of the Wee Free persuasion and, as such, want nothing to do with you and your Church's wanton ways. So, if you're touting for business, you've come to the wrong person. Is there anything else?' Her eyes stared at me with obvious suspicion and ill-disguised disapproval.

'I wondered how much you wanted for the mug in the

window – the one with the partridge on it,' I enquired.

She sniffed and, again showing her natural gift for ventrilo-
quism, she said, 'I think it's only right and fair that I point out
that it's not a partridge but is only a member of the partridge
family. It's a quail.' She retrieved it from the window. On
the back was a message that said *A PRESENT FROM THE
SCOTTISH HIGHLANDS*.

'They're hand-painted by a local artist but I think it's only
right and fair that I should point out that, when I say local, I
mean that in a secular way only. He is of the Jewish persuasion
and is not affiliated in any way with the owners of this establishment,' she declared, handing it over. 'I think it's only right and
fair to point out that, if you break it, we consider you've bought
it.'

Carefully, I took the mug in my hands. It was plain to see
why I was drawn to it. The painting of the bird was really
remarkable in its detail and the artist was obviously highly
skilled. Out of curiosity, I turned the mug upside down to see
that stamped on the bottom running round the rim was the
artist's name – *Alf Heyus*. Inexplicably, a shiver ran through
me. I felt as if I knew him but did not know how I knew him.
I made up my mind there and then to visit him.

I also made up my mind not to buy the mug, explaining to
her that it was only right and fair that, at six pounds ninety-
nine, it was too expensive.

The End

Also available:

RIKKI FULTON'S
REVEREND I.M. JOLLY

HOW I FOUND GOD
AND WHY HE WAS HIDING FROM ME

BY
TONY ROPER

Who is the mysterious felon stalking Rev Jolly? Is his beloved wife
Ephesia having an affair? Is Jolly about to lose his job? Find out
in the hilarious adventures of Scotland's best-loved minister.

Available from all good bookshops
or at www.blackandwhitepublishing.com